W9-AUE-463

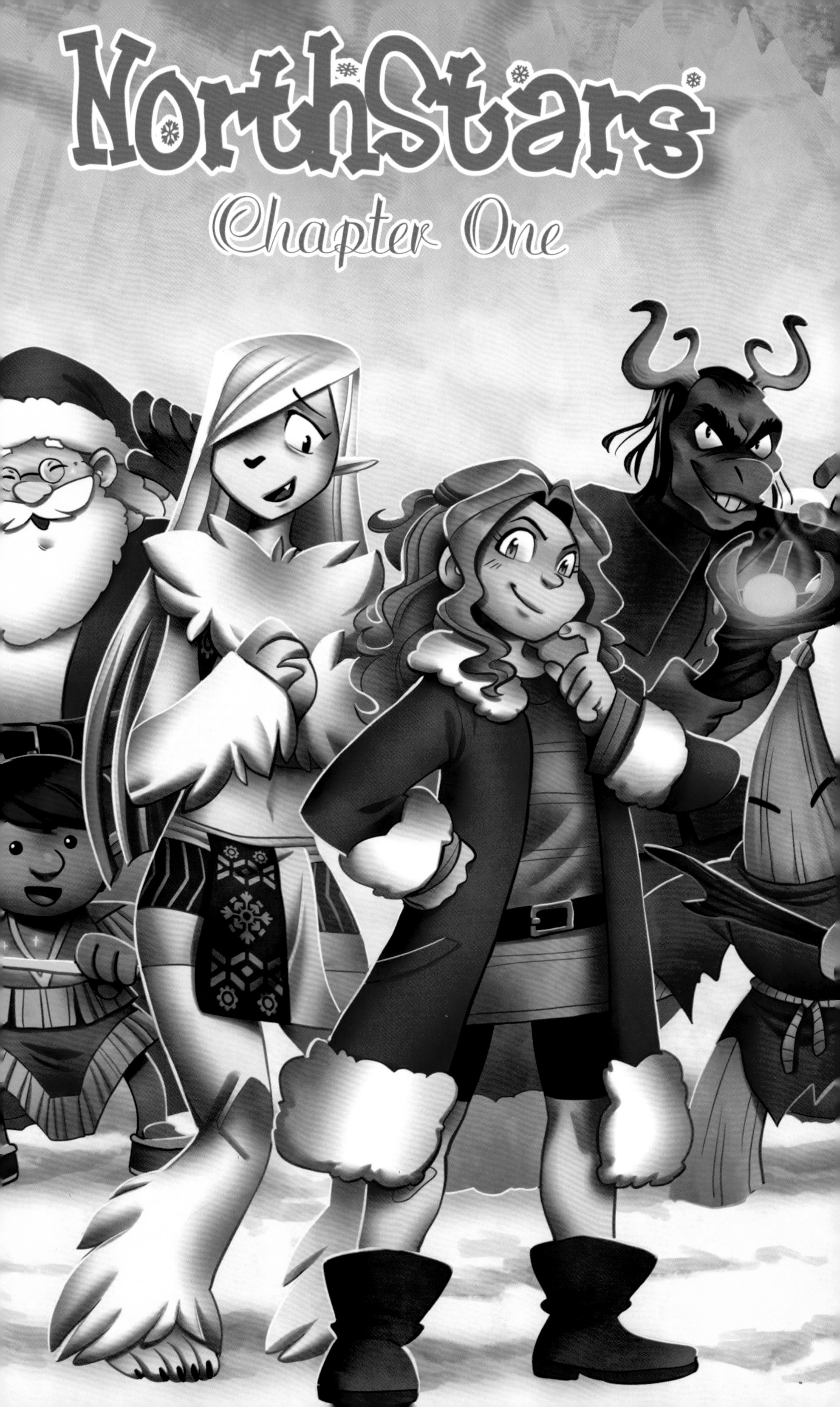
NorthStars
Chapter One

NorthStars

Story & Flatting
Jim & Haigen Shelley

Art, Colors & Letters
Anna Liisa Jones

ACTION LAB STAFF

Bryan Seaton
CEO & PUBLISHER

Shawn Gabborin
EDITOR IN CHIEF

Jason Martin
DANGER ZONE PUBLISHER

Chad Cicconi
SANTA'S ELF

Nicole D'Andria
MARKETING DIRECTOR/EDITOR

Jim Dietz
SOCIAL MEDIA DIRECTOR

Danielle Davidson
EXECUTIVE ADMINISTRATOR

Shawn Pryor
PRESIDENT OF CREATOR RELATIONS

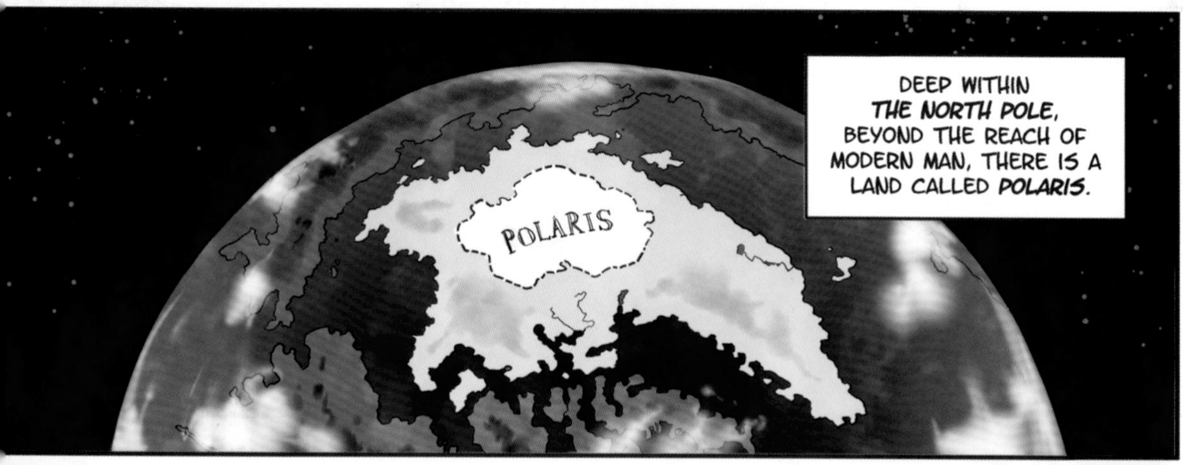
DEEP WITHIN
THE NORTH POLE,
BEYOND THE REACH OF
MODERN MAN, THERE IS A
LAND CALLED POLARIS.
POLARIS

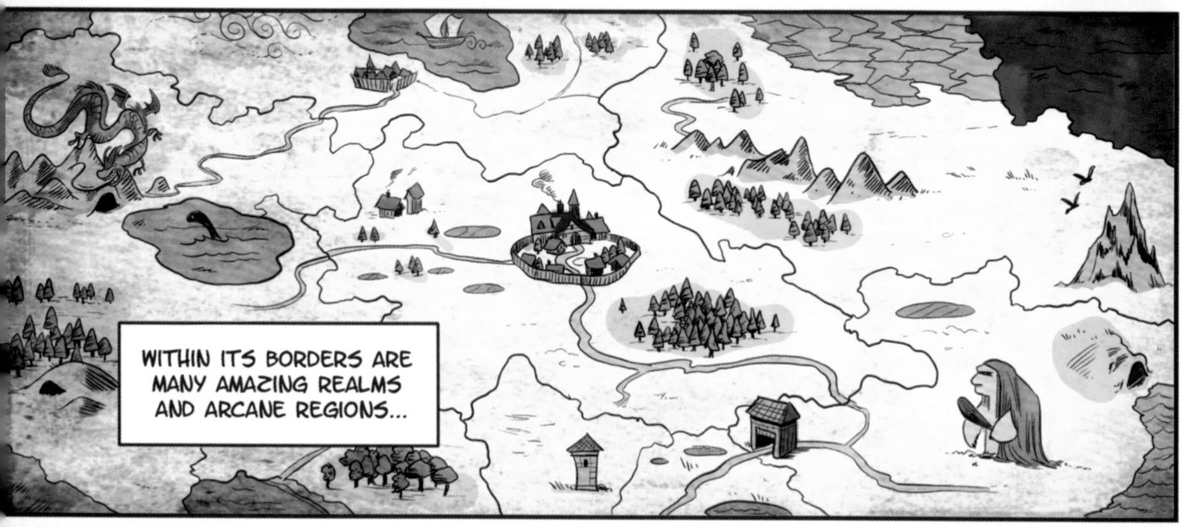
WITHIN ITS BORDERS ARE
MANY AMAZING REALMS
AND ARCANE REGIONS...

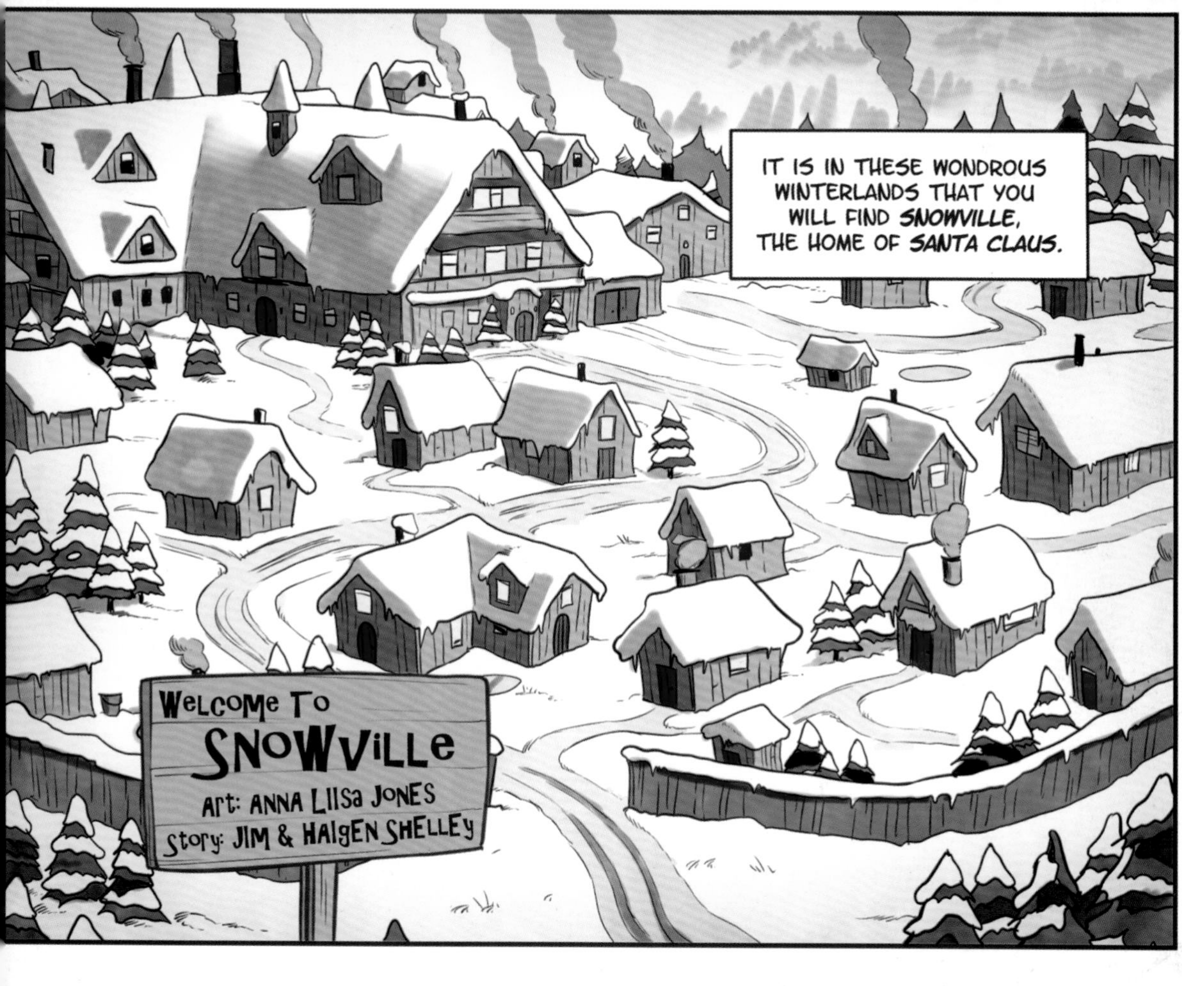
IT IS IN THESE WONDROUS
WINTERLANDS THAT YOU
WILL FIND SNOWVILLE,
THE HOME OF SANTA CLAUS.
Welcome To
SNOWVILLE
Art: ANNA LIISA JONES
Story: JIM & HAIGEN SHELLEY

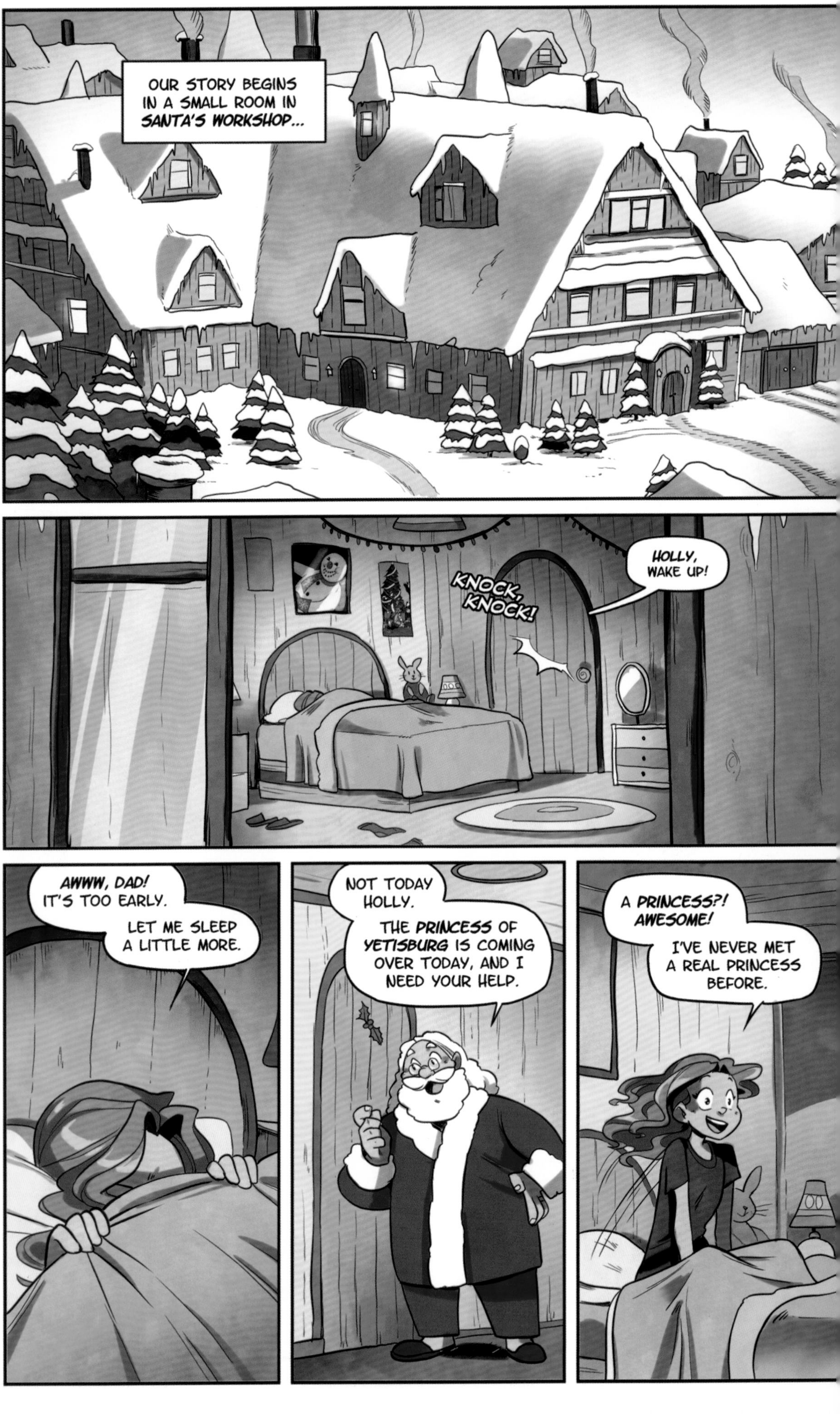
OUR STORY BEGINS IN A SMALL ROOM IN SANTA'S WORKSHOP...
KNOCK, KNOCK!
HOLLY, WAKE UP!
AWWW, DAD! IT'S TOO EARLY.
LET ME SLEEP A LITTLE MORE.
NOT TODAY HOLLY.
THE PRINCESS OF YETISBURG IS COMING OVER TODAY, AND I NEED YOUR HELP.
A PRINCESS?! AWESOME!
I'VE NEVER MET A REAL PRINCESS BEFORE.

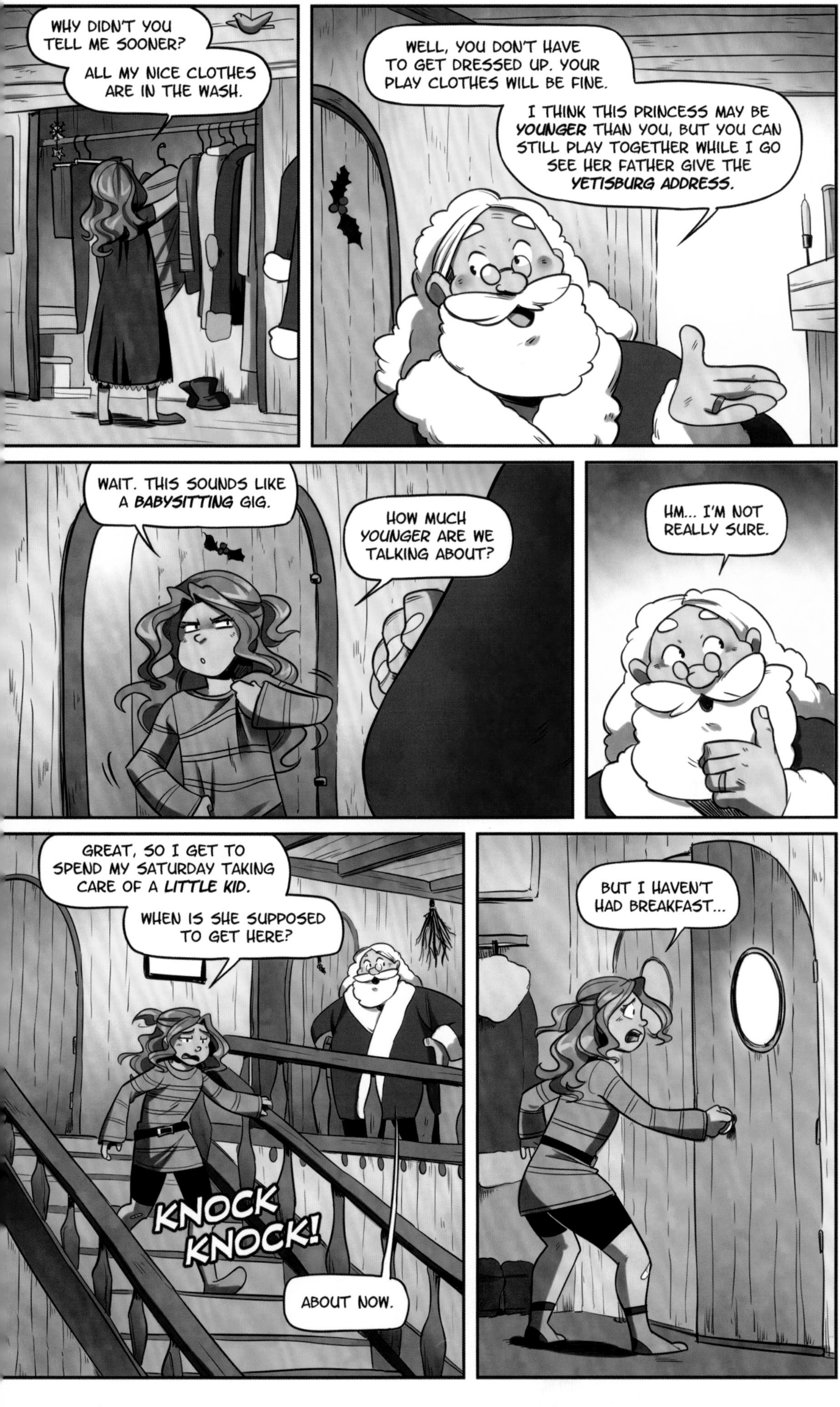

WHY DIDN'T YOU TELL ME SOONER?
ALL MY NICE CLOTHES ARE IN THE WASH.
WELL, YOU DON'T HAVE TO GET DRESSED UP. YOUR PLAY CLOTHES WILL BE FINE.
I THINK THIS PRINCESS MAY BE YOUNGER THAN YOU, BUT YOU CAN STILL PLAY TOGETHER WHILE I GO SEE HER FATHER GIVE THE YETISBURG ADDRESS.
WAIT. THIS SOUNDS LIKE A BABYSITTING GIG.
HOW MUCH YOUNGER ARE WE TALKING ABOUT?
HM... I'M NOT REALLY SURE.
GREAT, SO I GET TO SPEND MY SATURDAY TAKING CARE OF A LITTLE KID.
WHEN IS SHE SUPPOSED TO GET HERE?
KNOCK KNOCK!
ABOUT NOW.
BUT I HAVEN'T HAD BREAKFAST...

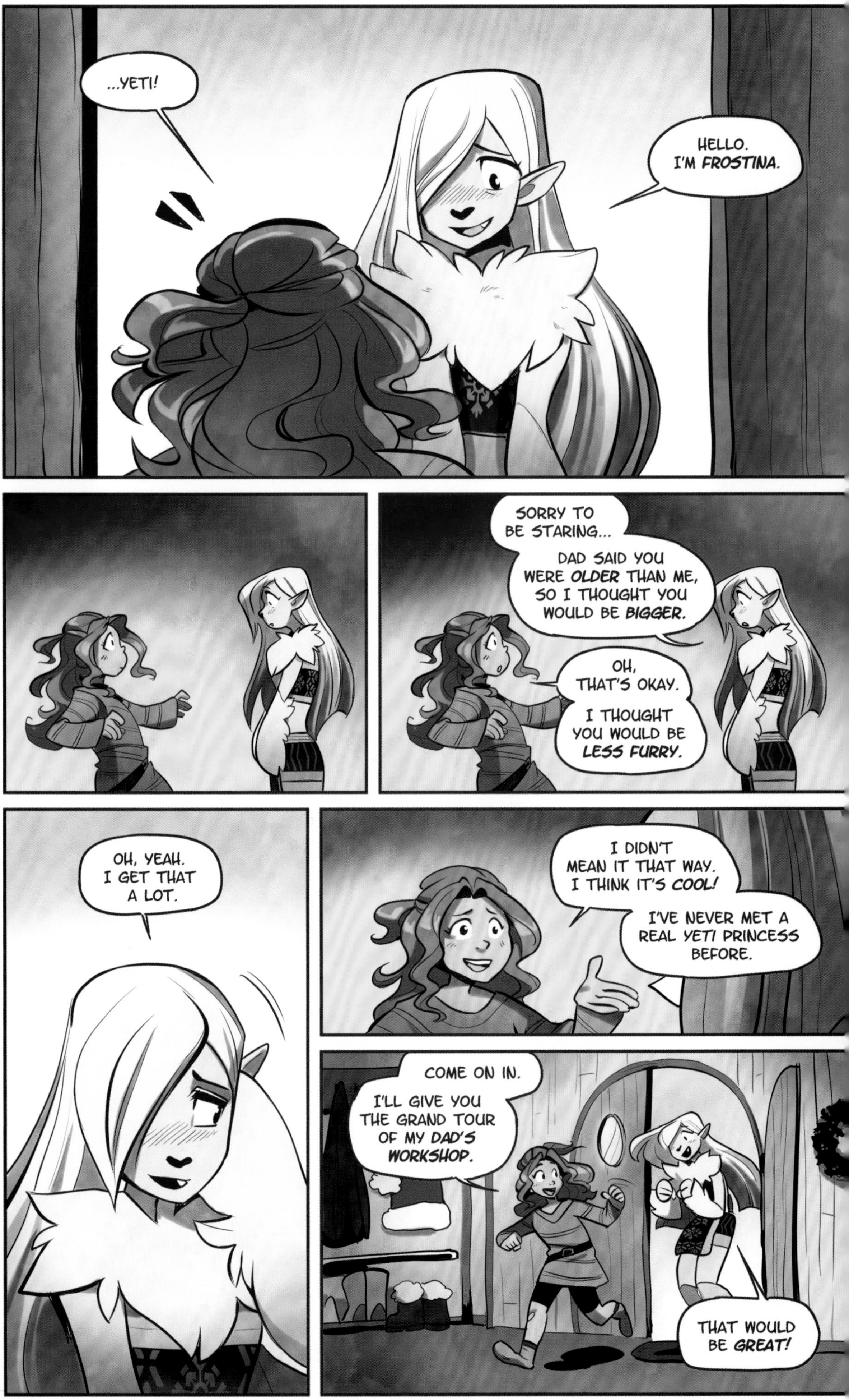
...YETI!
HELLO. I'M FROSTINA.
SORRY TO BE STARING...
DAD SAID YOU WERE OLDER THAN ME, SO I THOUGHT YOU WOULD BE BIGGER.
OH, THAT'S OKAY.
I THOUGHT YOU WOULD BE LESS FURRY.
OH, YEAH. I GET THAT A LOT.
I DIDN'T MEAN IT THAT WAY. I THINK IT'S COOL!
I'VE NEVER MET A REAL YETI PRINCESS BEFORE.
COME ON IN.
I'LL GIVE YOU THE GRAND TOUR OF MY DAD'S WORKSHOP.
THAT WOULD BE GREAT!

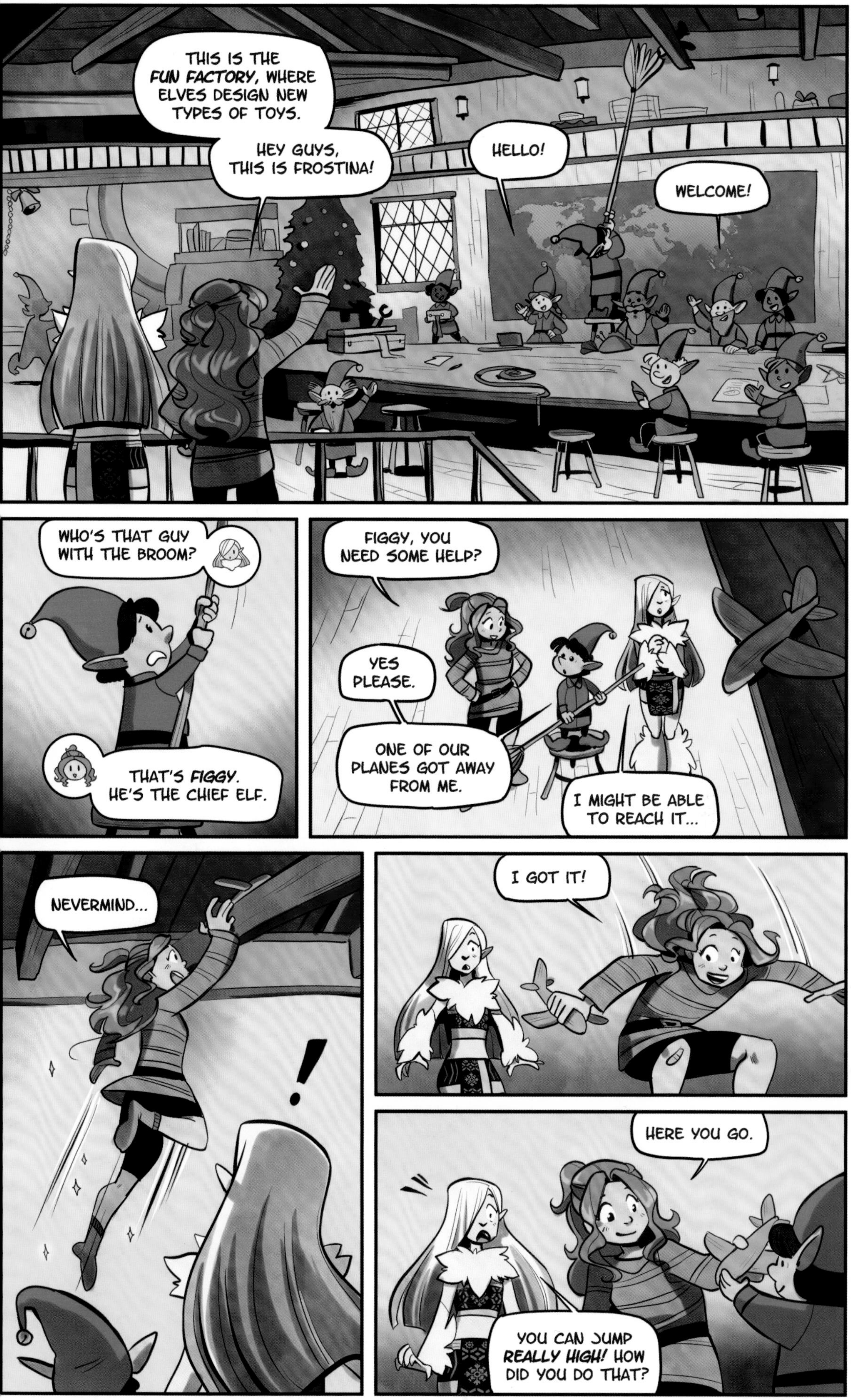
THIS IS THE FUN FACTORY, WHERE ELVES DESIGN NEW TYPES OF TOYS.
HEY GUYS, THIS IS FROSTINA!
HELLO!
WELCOME!
WHO'S THAT GUY WITH THE BROOM?
THAT'S FIGGY. HE'S THE CHIEF ELF.
FIGGY, YOU NEED SOME HELP?
YES PLEASE.
ONE OF OUR PLANES GOT AWAY FROM ME.
I MIGHT BE ABLE TO REACH IT...
NEVERMIND...
!
I GOT IT!
HERE YOU GO.
YOU CAN JUMP REALLY HIGH! HOW DID YOU DO THAT?

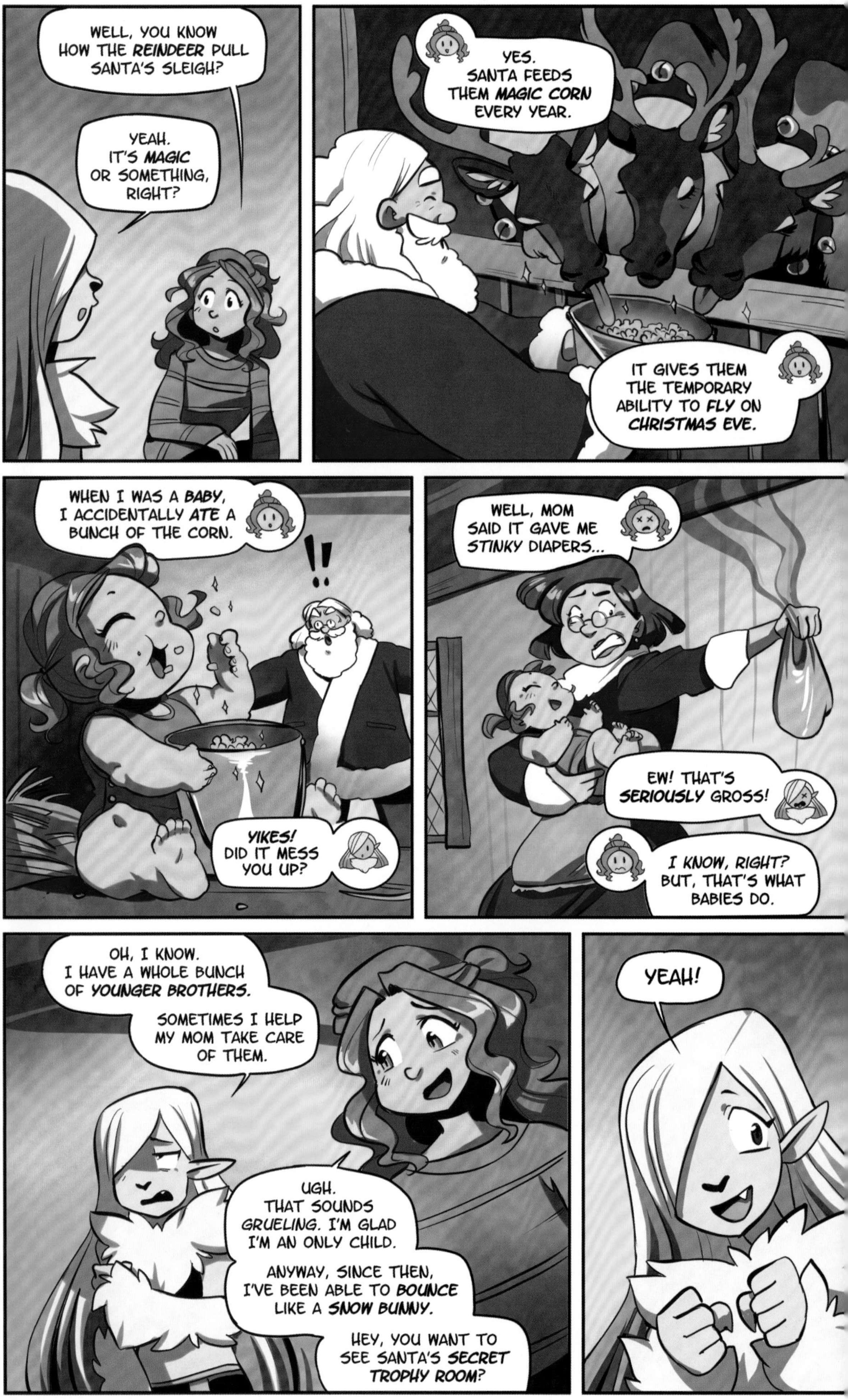

WELL, YOU KNOW HOW THE REINDEER PULL SANTA'S SLEIGH?
YEAH. IT'S MAGIC OR SOMETHING, RIGHT?
YES. SANTA FEEDS THEM MAGIC CORN EVERY YEAR.
IT GIVES THEM THE TEMPORARY ABILITY TO FLY ON CHRISTMAS EVE.
WHEN I WAS A BABY, I ACCIDENTALLY ATE A BUNCH OF THE CORN.
!!
YIKES! DID IT MESS YOU UP?
WELL, MOM SAID IT GAVE ME STINKY DIAPERS...
EW! THAT'S SERIOUSLY GROSS!
I KNOW, RIGHT? BUT, THAT'S WHAT BABIES DO.
OH, I KNOW. I HAVE A WHOLE BUNCH OF YOUNGER BROTHERS.
SOMETIMES I HELP MY MOM TAKE CARE OF THEM.
UGH. THAT SOUNDS GRUELING. I'M GLAD I'M AN ONLY CHILD.
ANYWAY, SINCE THEN, I'VE BEEN ABLE TO BOUNCE LIKE A SNOW BUNNY.
HEY, YOU WANT TO SEE SANTA'S SECRET TROPHY ROOM?
YEAH!

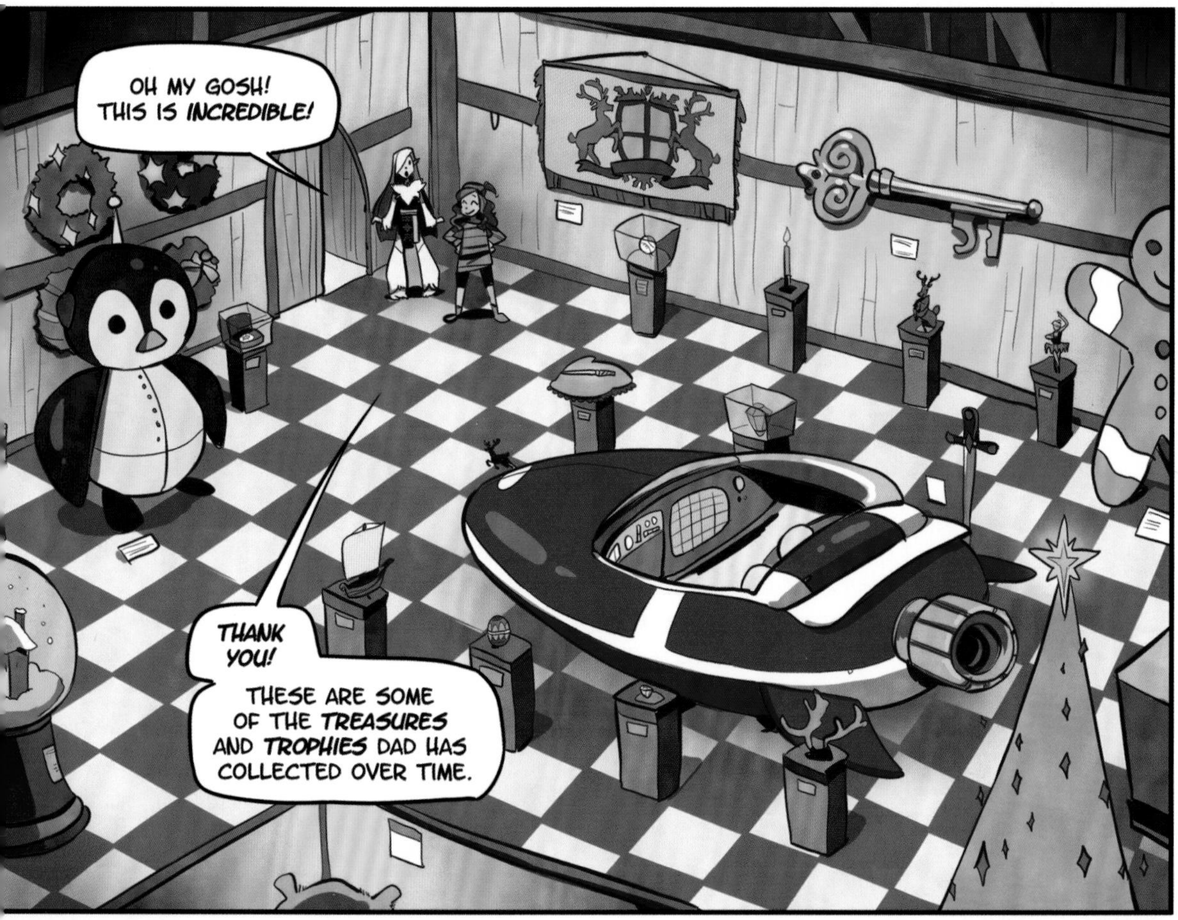
OH MY GOSH! THIS IS INCREDIBLE!
THANK YOU!
THESE ARE SOME OF THE TREASURES AND TROPHIES DAD HAS COLLECTED OVER TIME.

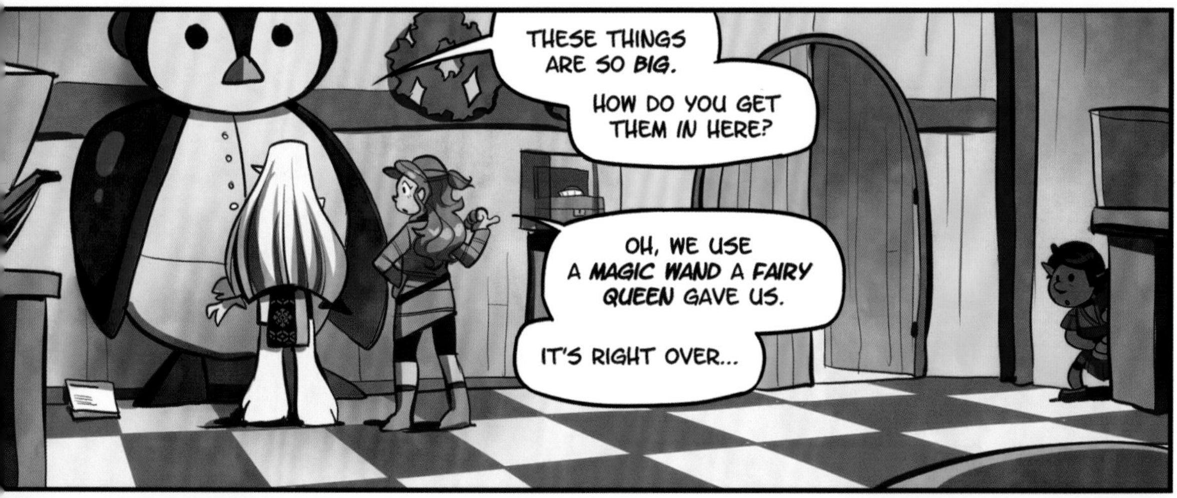
THESE THINGS ARE SO BIG.
HOW DO YOU GET THEM IN HERE?
OH, WE USE A MAGIC WAND A FAIRY QUEEN GAVE US.
IT'S RIGHT OVER...

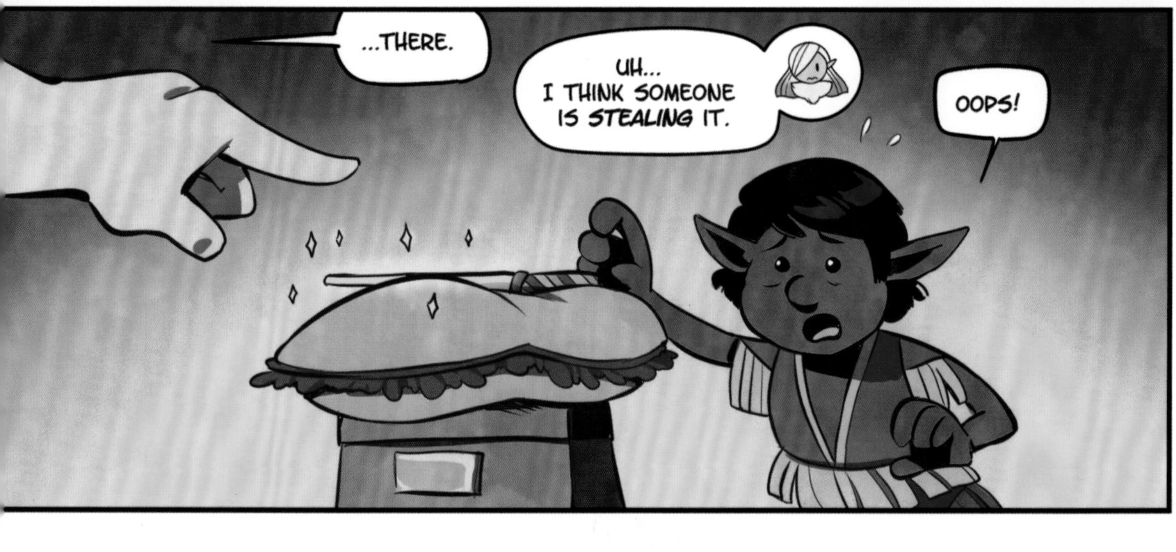
...THERE.
UH... I THINK SOMEONE IS STEALING IT.
OOPS!

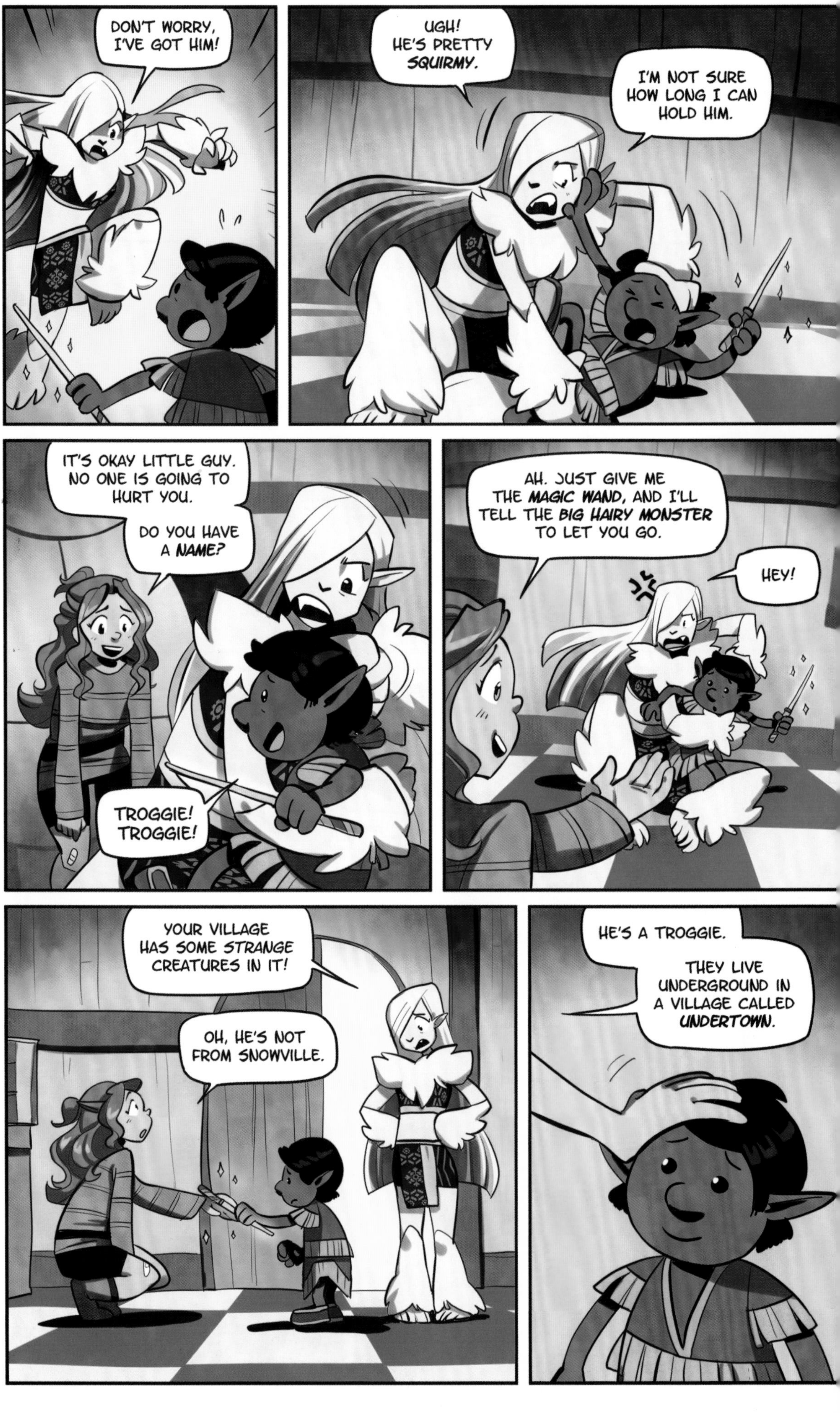

DON'T WORRY, I'VE GOT HIM!
UGH! HE'S PRETTY SQUIRMY.
I'M NOT SURE HOW LONG I CAN HOLD HIM.
IT'S OKAY LITTLE GUY. NO ONE IS GOING TO HURT YOU.
DO YOU HAVE A NAME?
TROGGIE! TROGGIE!
AH. JUST GIVE ME THE MAGIC WAND, AND I'LL TELL THE BIG HAIRY MONSTER TO LET YOU GO.
HEY!
YOUR VILLAGE HAS SOME STRANGE CREATURES IN IT!
OH, HE'S NOT FROM SNOWVILLE.
HE'S A TROGGIE.
THEY LIVE UNDERGROUND IN A VILLAGE CALLED UNDERTOWN.

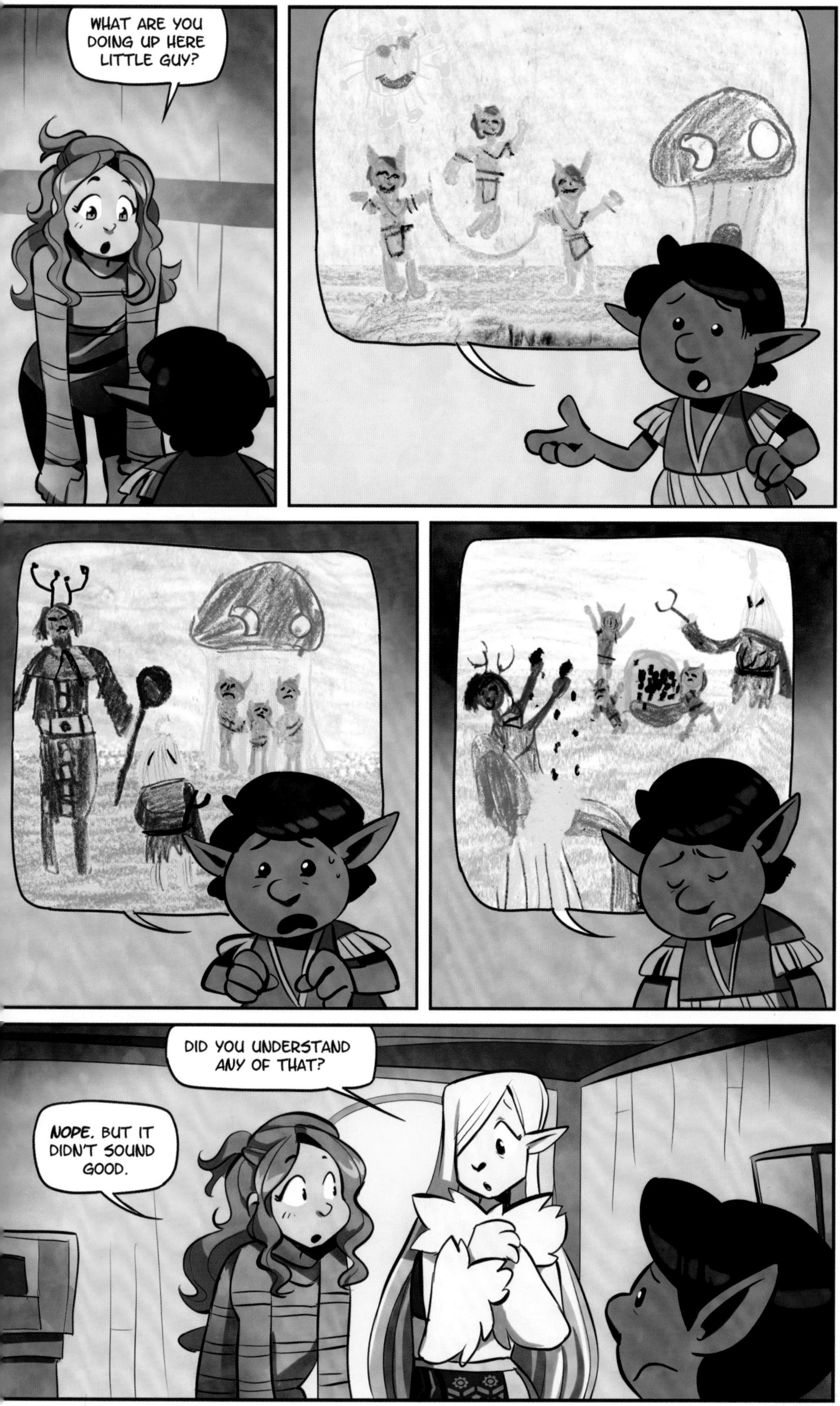
WHAT ARE YOU DOING UP HERE LITTLE GUY?
DID YOU UNDERSTAND ANY OF THAT?
NOPE. BUT IT DIDN'T SOUND GOOD.

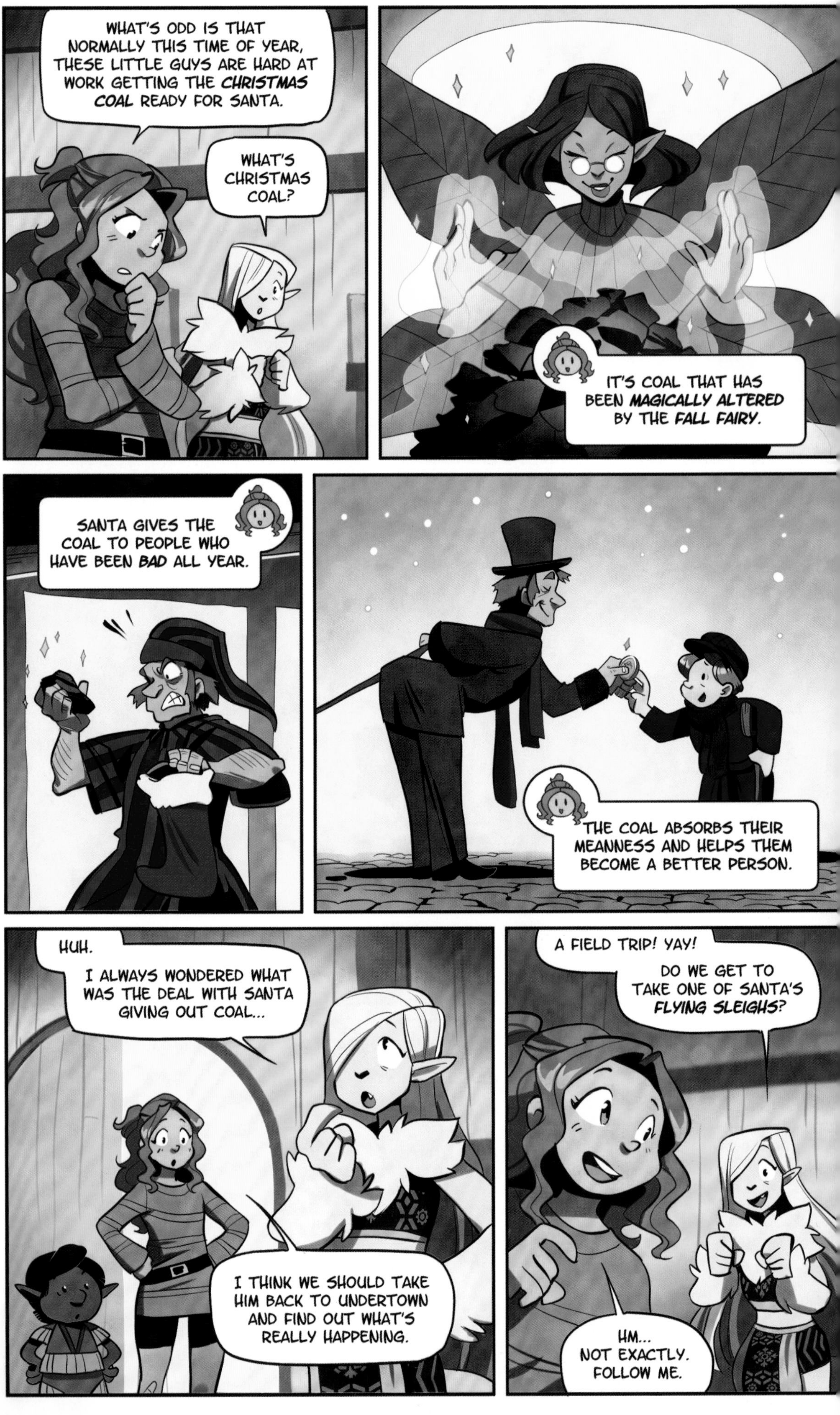
WHAT'S ODD IS THAT NORMALLY THIS TIME OF YEAR, THESE LITTLE GUYS ARE HARD AT WORK GETTING THE CHRISTMAS COAL READY FOR SANTA.
WHAT'S CHRISTMAS COAL?
IT'S COAL THAT HAS BEEN MAGICALLY ALTERED BY THE FALL FAIRY.
SANTA GIVES THE COAL TO PEOPLE WHO HAVE BEEN BAD ALL YEAR.
THE COAL ABSORBS THEIR MEANNESS AND HELPS THEM BECOME A BETTER PERSON.
HUH.
I ALWAYS WONDERED WHAT WAS THE DEAL WITH SANTA GIVING OUT COAL...
I THINK WE SHOULD TAKE HIM BACK TO UNDERTOWN AND FIND OUT WHAT'S REALLY HAPPENING.
A FIELD TRIP! YAY!
DO WE GET TO TAKE ONE OF SANTA'S FLYING SLEIGHS?
HM... NOT EXACTLY. FOLLOW ME.

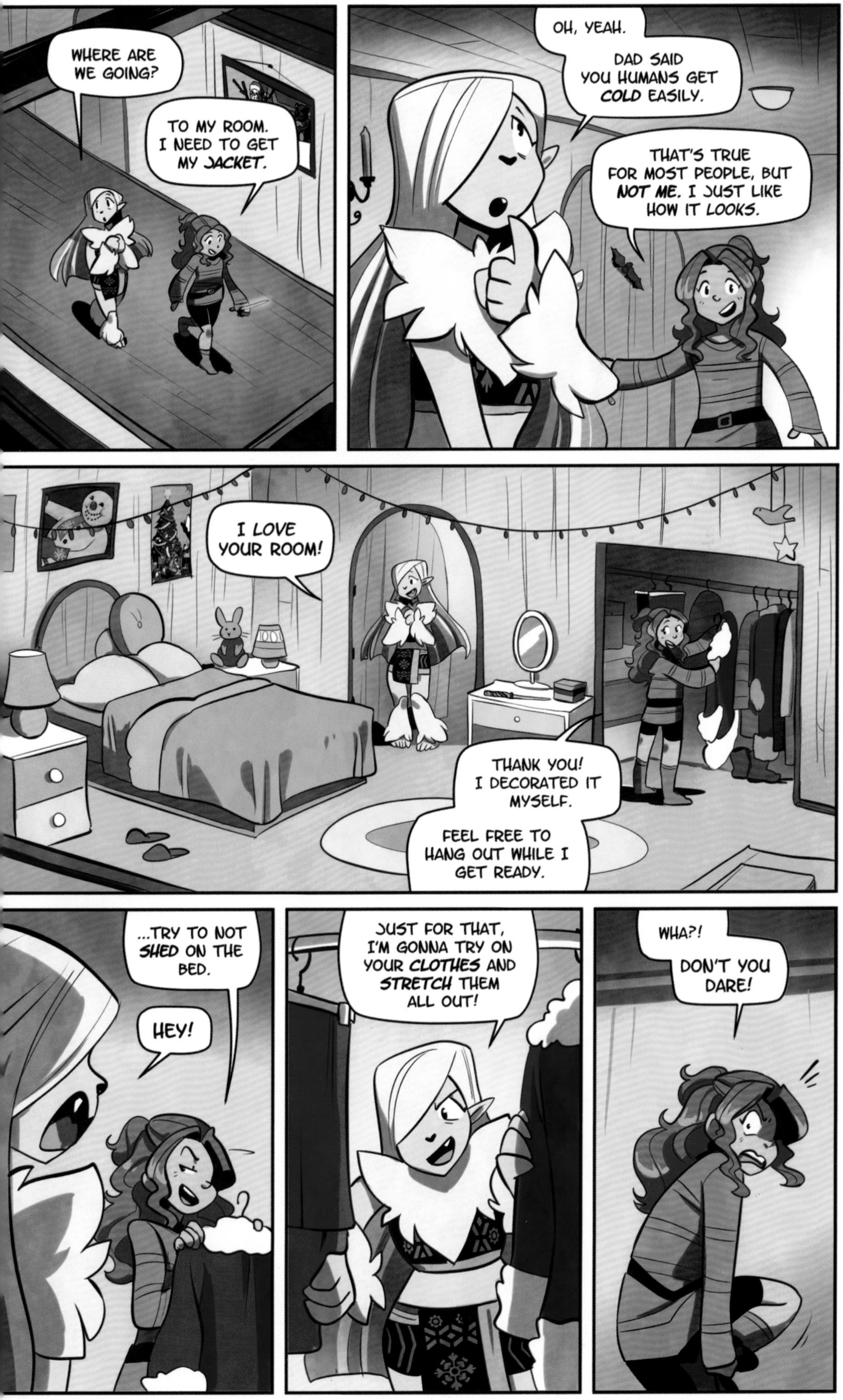
WHERE ARE WE GOING?
TO MY ROOM. I NEED TO GET MY JACKET.
OH, YEAH.
DAD SAID YOU HUMANS GET COLD EASILY.
THAT'S TRUE FOR MOST PEOPLE, BUT NOT ME. I JUST LIKE HOW IT LOOKS.
I LOVE YOUR ROOM!
THANK YOU! I DECORATED IT MYSELF.
FEEL FREE TO HANG OUT WHILE I GET READY.
...TRY TO NOT SHED ON THE BED.
HEY!
JUST FOR THAT, I'M GONNA TRY ON YOUR CLOTHES AND STRETCH THEM ALL OUT!
WHA?!
DON'T YOU DARE!

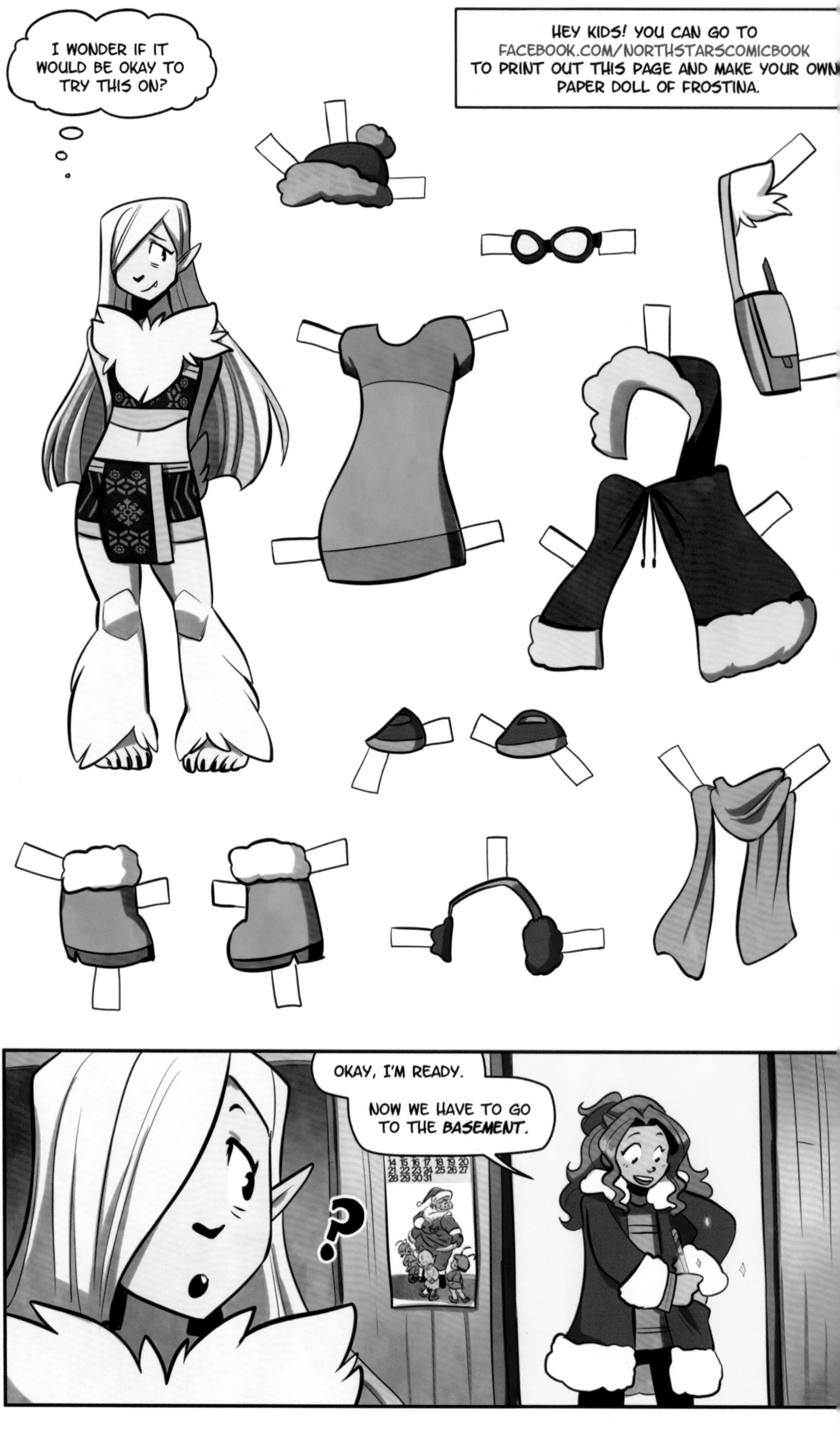
I WONDER IF IT WOULD BE OKAY TO TRY THIS ON?
HEY KIDS! YOU CAN GO TO FACEBOOK.COM/NORTHSTARSCOMICBOOK TO PRINT OUT THIS PAGE AND MAKE YOUR OWN PAPER DOLL OF FROSTINA.
OKAY, I'M READY.
NOW WE HAVE TO GO TO THE *BASEMENT*.
?

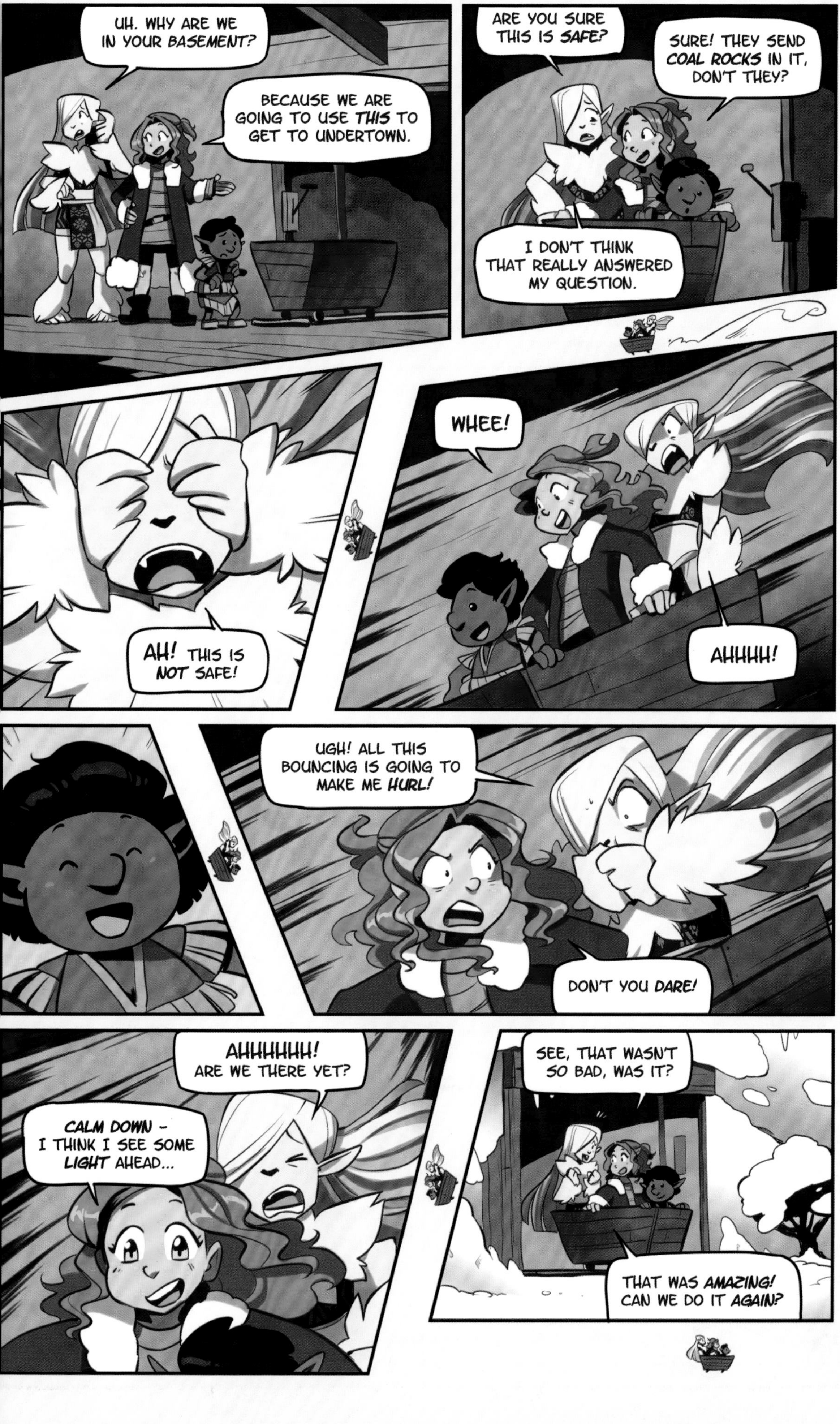
UH. WHY ARE WE IN YOUR BASEMENT?
BECAUSE WE ARE GOING TO USE THIS TO GET TO UNDERTOWN.
ARE YOU SURE THIS IS SAFE?
SURE! THEY SEND COAL ROCKS IN IT, DON'T THEY?
I DON'T THINK THAT REALLY ANSWERED MY QUESTION.
AH! THIS IS NOT SAFE!
WHEE!
AHHHH!
UGH! ALL THIS BOUNCING IS GOING TO MAKE ME HURL!
DON'T YOU DARE!
AHHHHHH! ARE WE THERE YET?
CALM DOWN - I THINK I SEE SOME LIGHT AHEAD...
SEE, THAT WASN'T SO BAD, WAS IT?
THAT WAS AMAZING! CAN WE DO IT AGAIN?

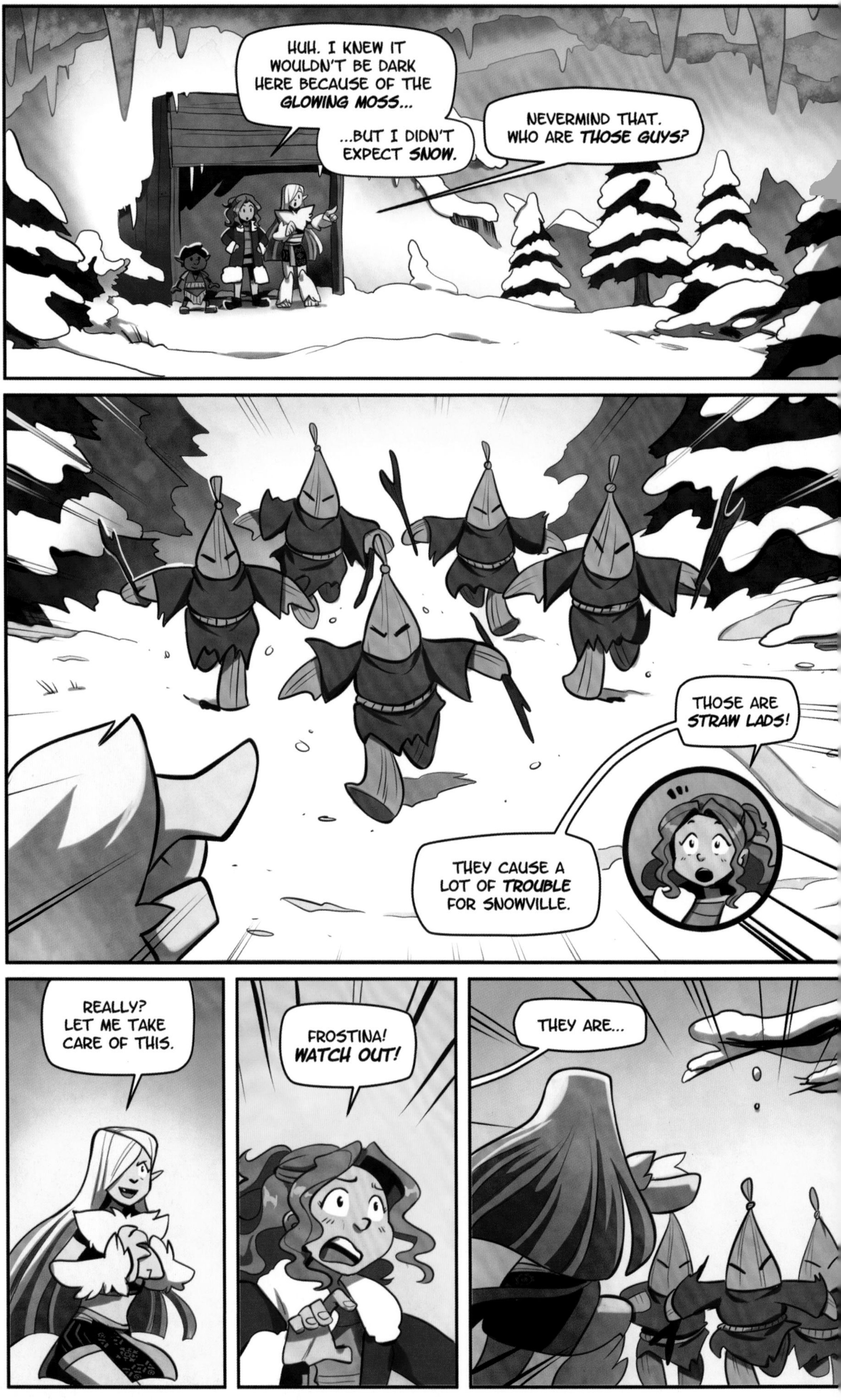

HUH. I KNEW IT WOULDN'T BE DARK HERE BECAUSE OF THE GLOWING MOSS...
...BUT I DIDN'T EXPECT SNOW.
NEVERMIND THAT. WHO ARE THOSE GUYS?
THOSE ARE STRAW LADS!
THEY CAUSE A LOT OF TROUBLE FOR SNOWVILLE.
REALLY? LET ME TAKE CARE OF THIS.
FROSTINA! WATCH OUT!
THEY ARE...

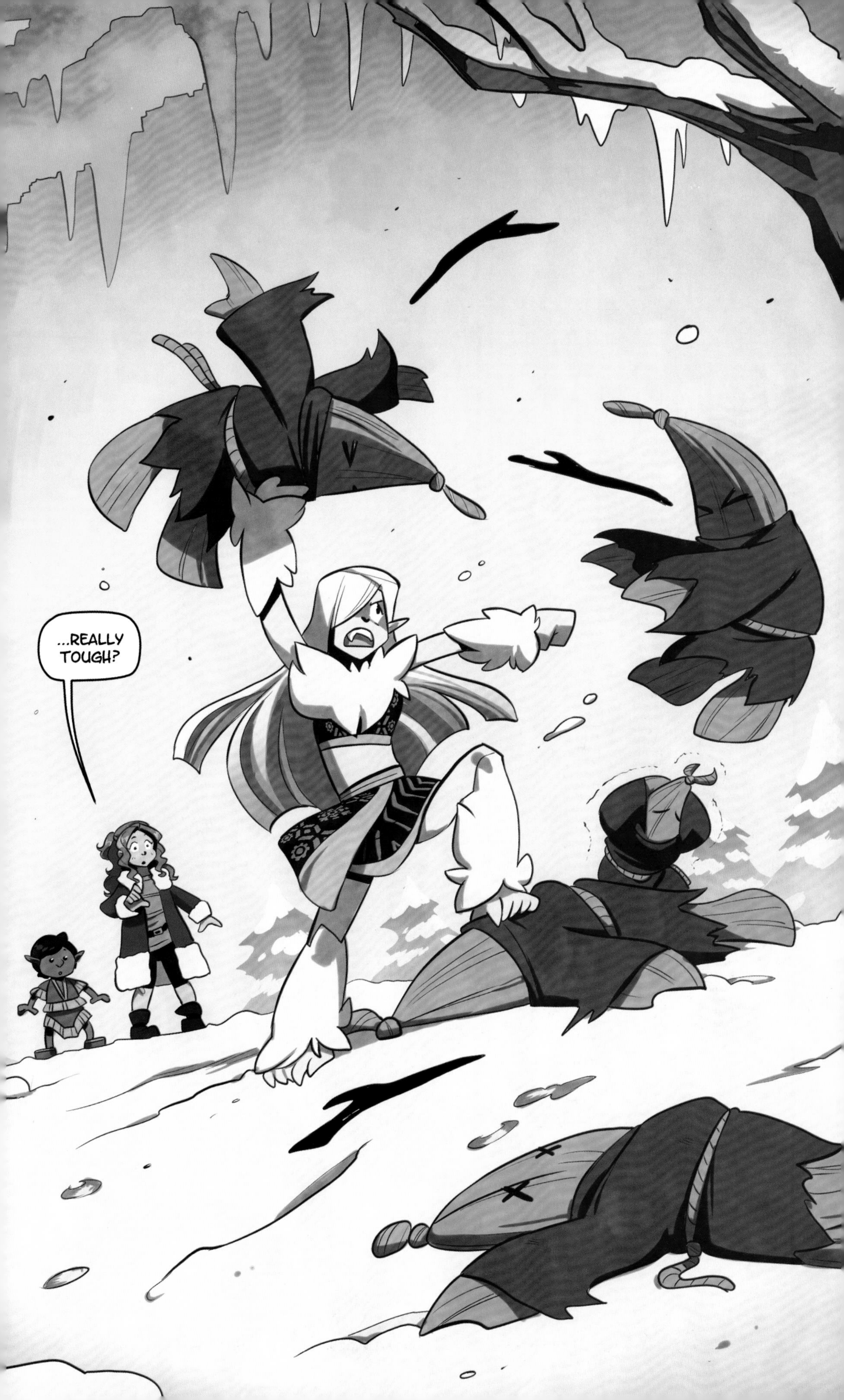
...REALLY TOUGH?

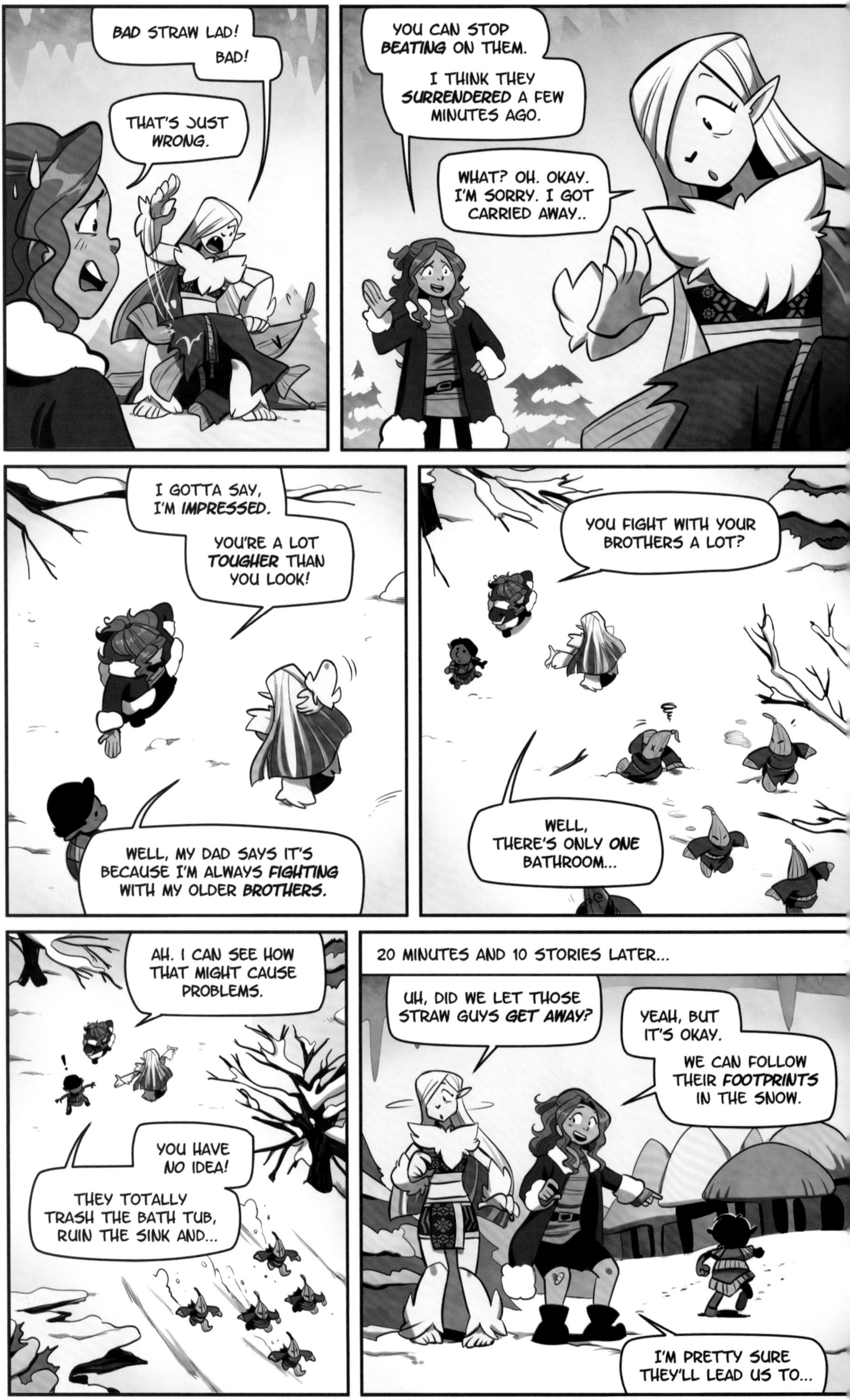
BAD STRAW LAD!
BAD!
THAT'S JUST WRONG.
YOU CAN STOP BEATING ON THEM.
I THINK THEY SURRENDERED A FEW MINUTES AGO.
WHAT? OH. OKAY. I'M SORRY. I GOT CARRIED AWAY..
I GOTTA SAY, I'M IMPRESSED.
YOU'RE A LOT TOUGHER THAN YOU LOOK!
WELL, MY DAD SAYS IT'S BECAUSE I'M ALWAYS FIGHTING WITH MY OLDER BROTHERS.
YOU FIGHT WITH YOUR BROTHERS A LOT?
WELL, THERE'S ONLY ONE BATHROOM...
AH. I CAN SEE HOW THAT MIGHT CAUSE PROBLEMS.
YOU HAVE NO IDEA!
THEY TOTALLY TRASH THE BATH TUB, RUIN THE SINK AND...
20 MINUTES AND 10 STORIES LATER...
UH, DID WE LET THOSE STRAW GUYS GET AWAY?
YEAH, BUT IT'S OKAY.
WE CAN FOLLOW THEIR FOOTPRINTS IN THE SNOW.
I'M PRETTY SURE THEY'LL LEAD US TO...

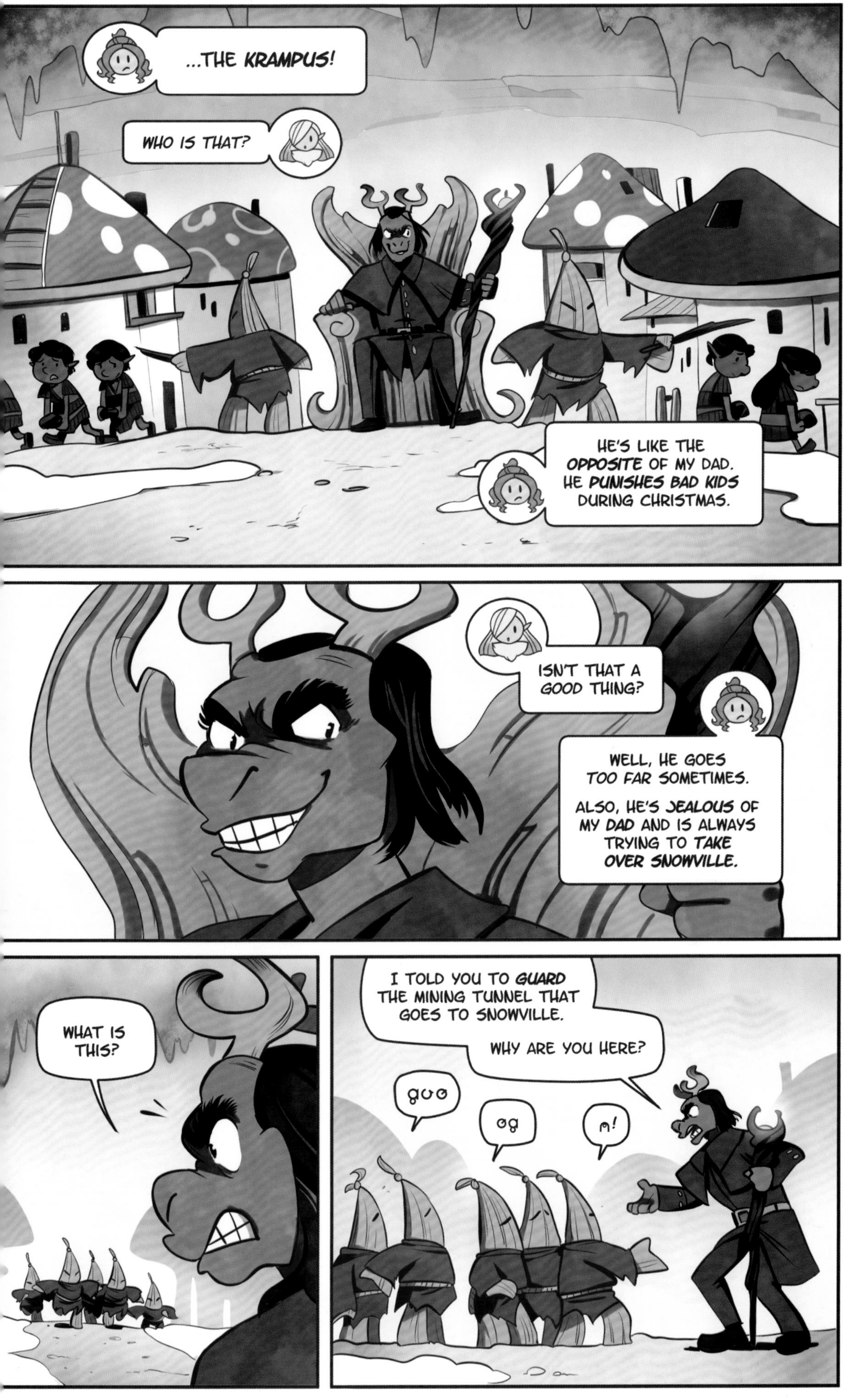
...THE KRAMPUS!
WHO IS THAT?
HE'S LIKE THE OPPOSITE OF MY DAD. HE PUNISHES BAD KIDS DURING CHRISTMAS.
ISN'T THAT A GOOD THING?
WELL, HE GOES TOO FAR SOMETIMES.
ALSO, HE'S JEALOUS OF MY DAD AND IS ALWAYS TRYING TO TAKE OVER SNOWVILLE.
WHAT IS THIS?
I TOLD YOU TO GUARD THE MINING TUNNEL THAT GOES TO SNOWVILLE.
WHY ARE YOU HERE?
guo
og
m!

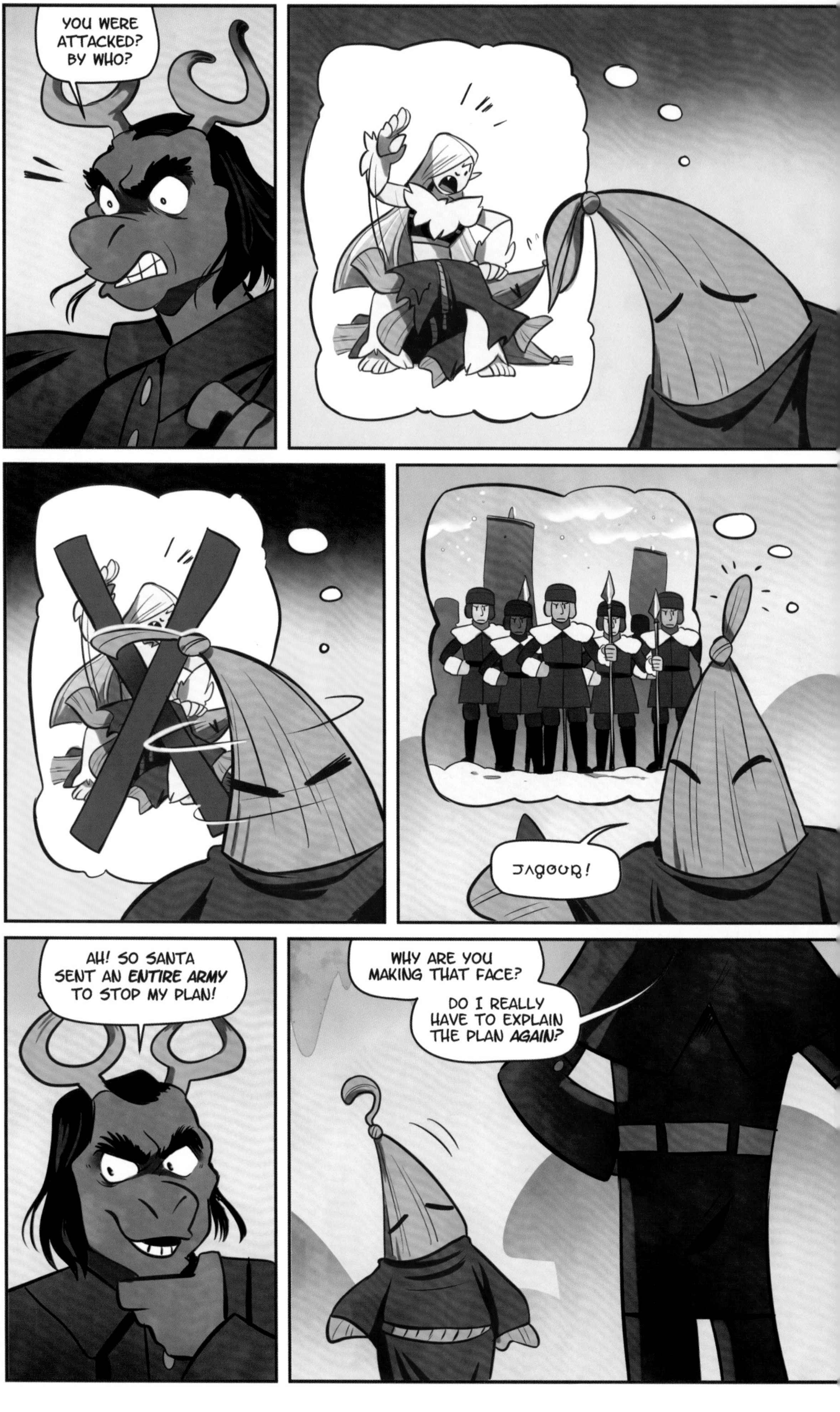
YOU WERE ATTACKED? BY WHO?
AH! SO SANTA SENT AN *ENTIRE ARMY* TO STOP MY PLAN!
WHY ARE YOU MAKING THAT FACE?
DO I REALLY HAVE TO EXPLAIN THE PLAN *AGAIN*?

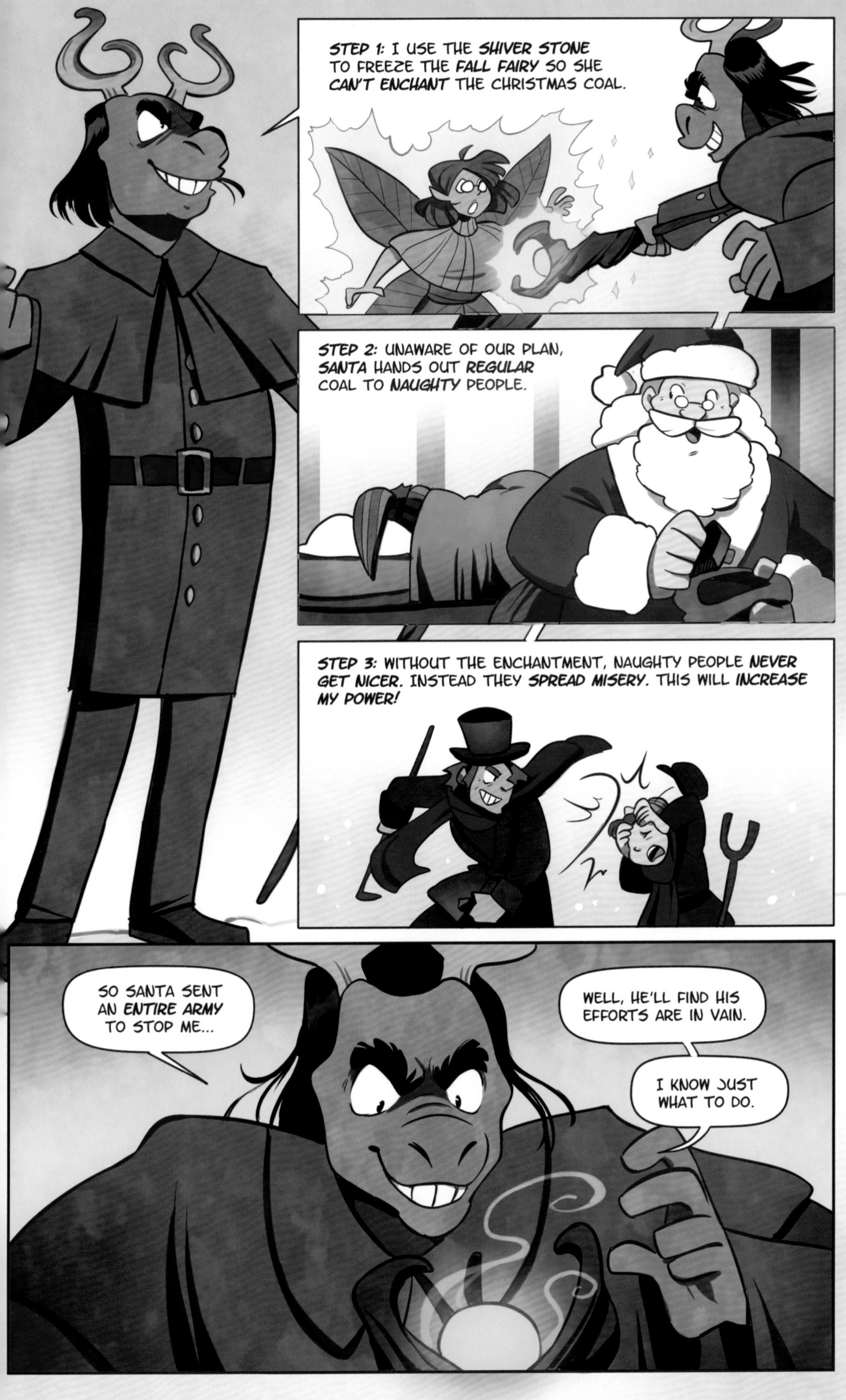
STEP 1: I USE THE SHIVER STONE TO FREEZE THE FALL FAIRY SO SHE CAN'T ENCHANT THE CHRISTMAS COAL.
STEP 2: UNAWARE OF OUR PLAN, SANTA HANDS OUT REGULAR COAL TO NAUGHTY PEOPLE.
STEP 3: WITHOUT THE ENCHANTMENT, NAUGHTY PEOPLE NEVER GET NICER. INSTEAD THEY SPREAD MISERY. THIS WILL INCREASE MY POWER!
SO SANTA SENT AN ENTIRE ARMY TO STOP ME...
WELL, HE'LL FIND HIS EFFORTS ARE IN VAIN.
I KNOW JUST WHAT TO DO.

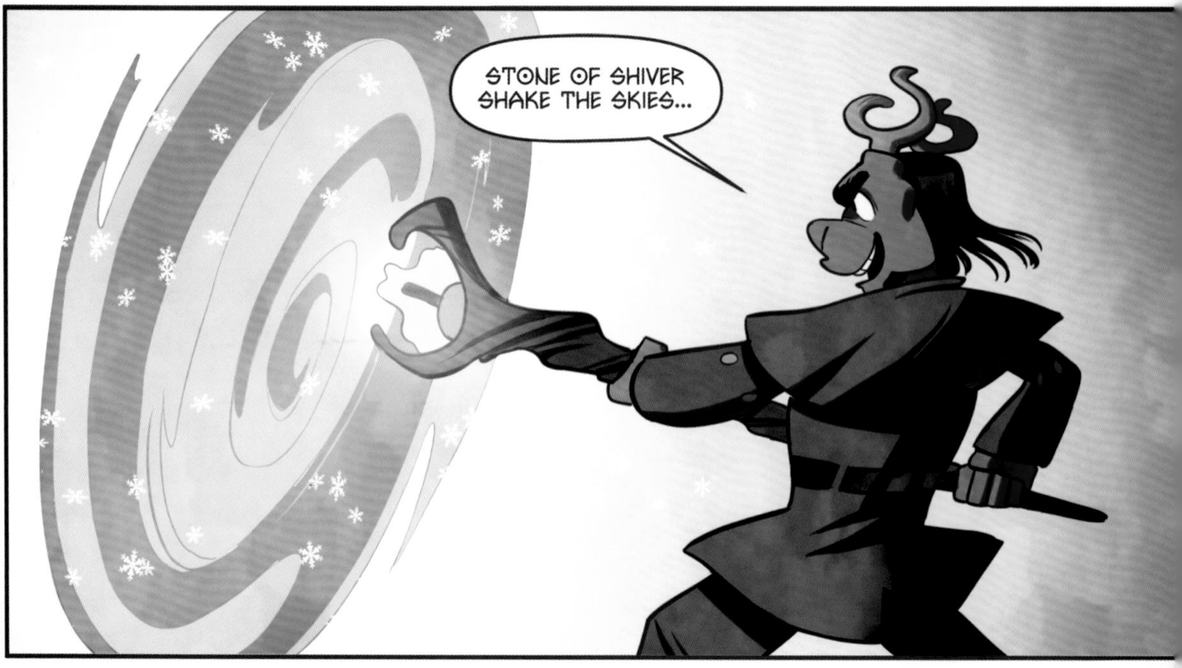
STONE OF SHIVER SHAKE THE SKIES...

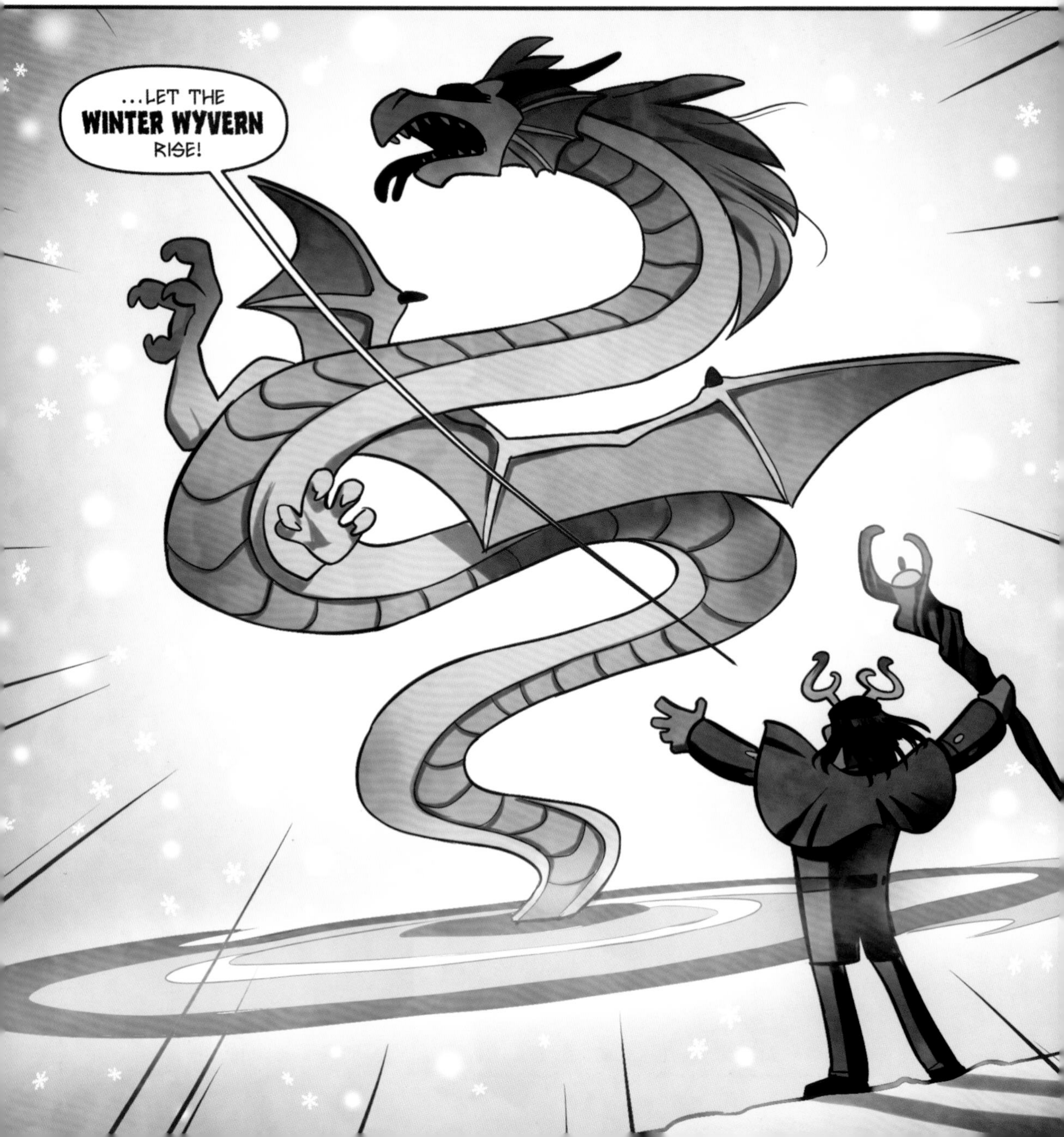
...LET THE WINTER WYVERN RISE!

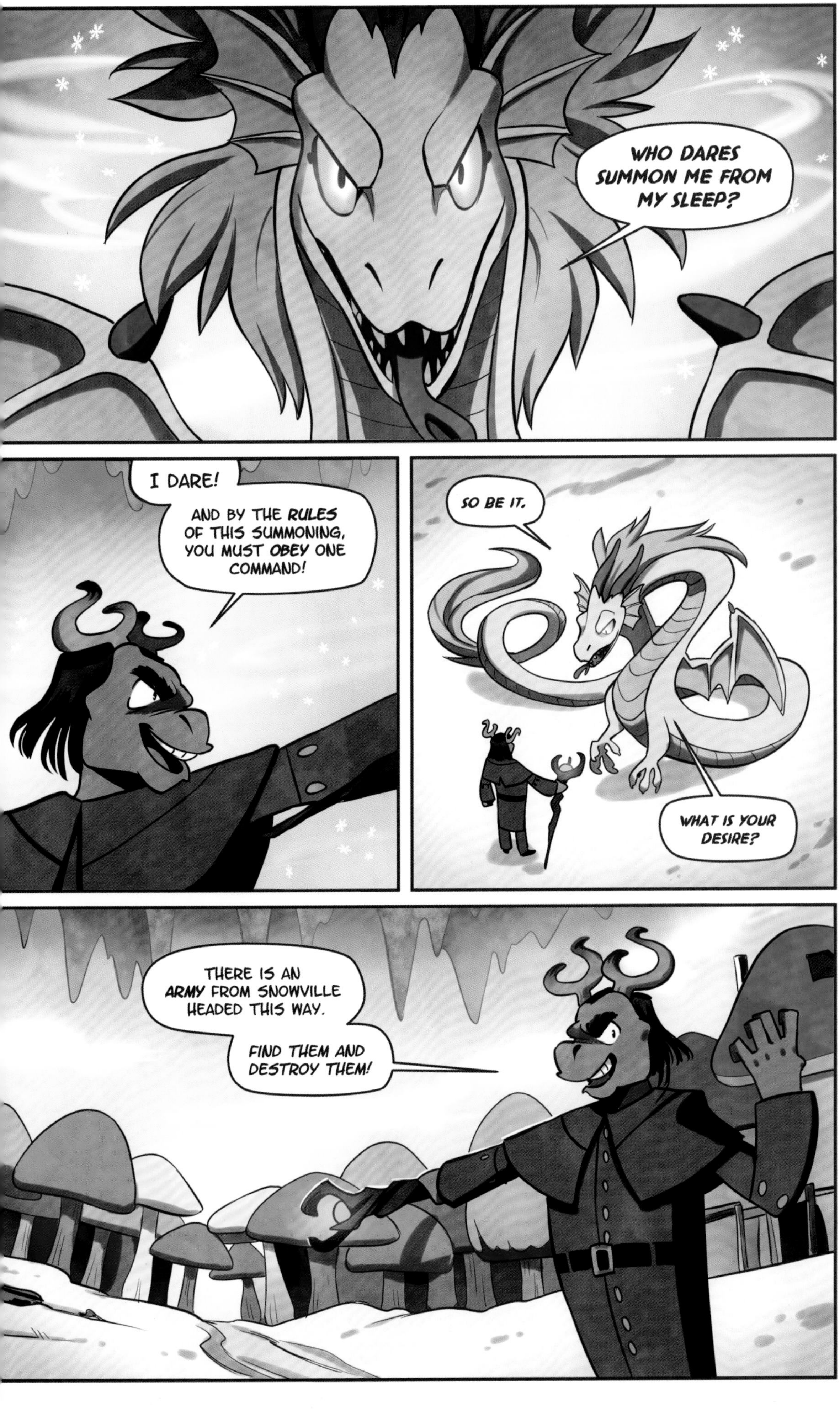
WHO DARES SUMMON ME FROM MY SLEEP?
I DARE!
AND BY THE RULES OF THIS SUMMONING, YOU MUST OBEY ONE COMMAND!
SO BE IT.
WHAT IS YOUR DESIRE?
THERE IS AN ARMY FROM SNOWVILLE HEADED THIS WAY.
FIND THEM AND DESTROY THEM!

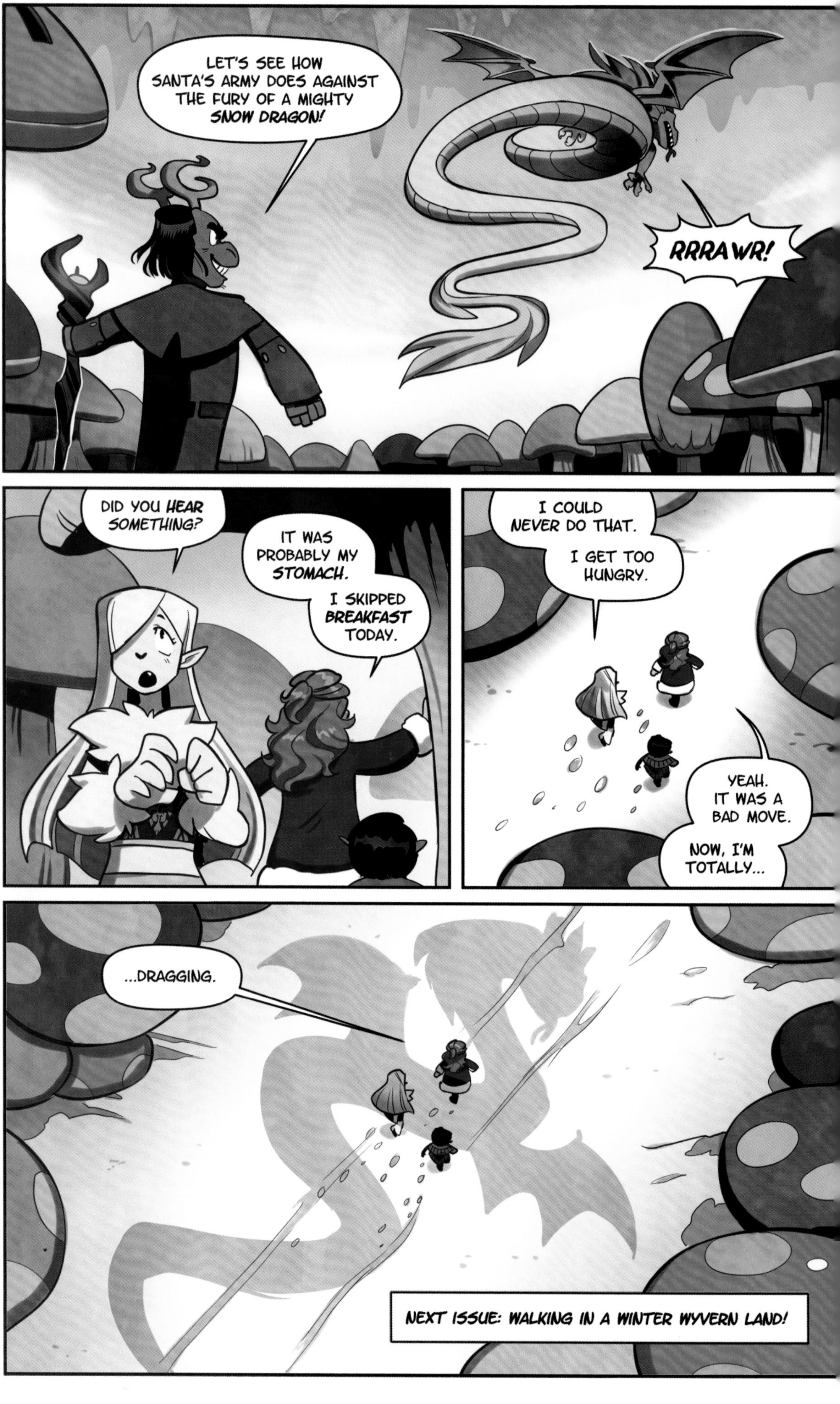
LET'S SEE HOW SANTA'S ARMY DOES AGAINST THE FURY OF A MIGHTY SNOW DRAGON!
RRRAWR!
DID YOU HEAR SOMETHING?
IT WAS PROBABLY MY STOMACH.
I SKIPPED BREAKFAST TODAY.
I COULD NEVER DO THAT.
I GET TOO HUNGRY.
YEAH. IT WAS A BAD MOVE.
NOW, I'M TOTALLY...
...DRAGGING.
NEXT ISSUE: WALKING IN A WINTER WYVERN LAND!

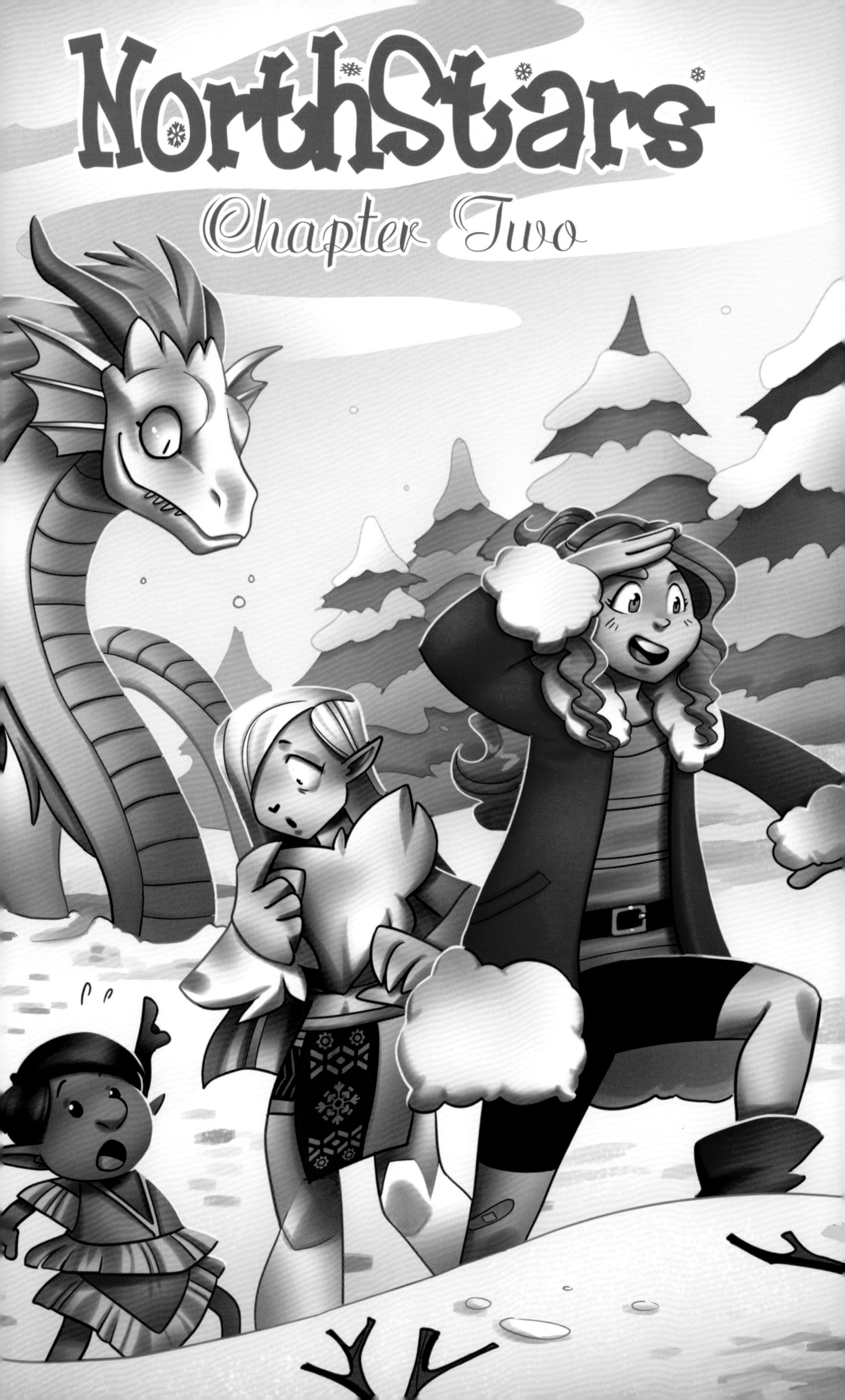
NorthStars
Chapter Two

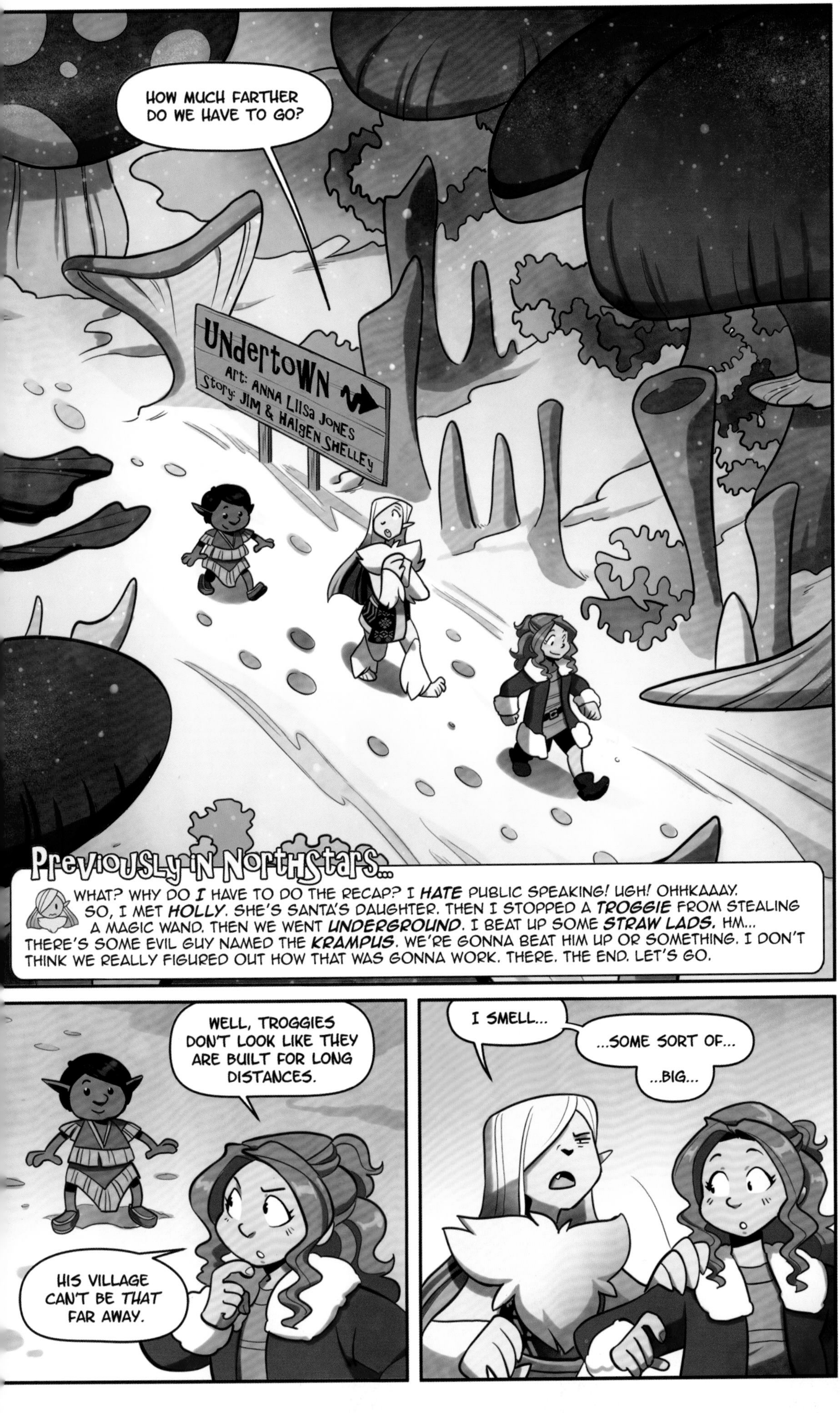
HOW MUCH FARTHER DO WE HAVE TO GO?
UNdertowN
Art: ANNA LIISA JONES
Story: JIM & HAIGEN SHELLEY
Previously in NorthStars...
WHAT? WHY DO *I* HAVE TO DO THE RECAP? I *HATE* PUBLIC SPEAKING! UGH! OHHKAAAY. SO, I MET *HOLLY*. SHE'S SANTA'S DAUGHTER. THEN I STOPPED A *TROGGIE* FROM STEALING A MAGIC WAND. THEN WE WENT *UNDERGROUND*. I BEAT UP SOME *STRAW LADS.* HM... THERE'S SOME EVIL GUY NAMED THE *KRAMPUS*. WE'RE GONNA BEAT HIM UP OR SOMETHING. I DON'T THINK WE REALLY FIGURED OUT HOW THAT WAS GONNA WORK. THERE. THE END. LET'S GO.
WELL, TROGGIES DON'T LOOK LIKE THEY ARE BUILT FOR LONG DISTANCES.
HIS VILLAGE CAN'T BE *THAT* FAR AWAY.
I SMELL...
...SOME SORT OF...
...BIG...

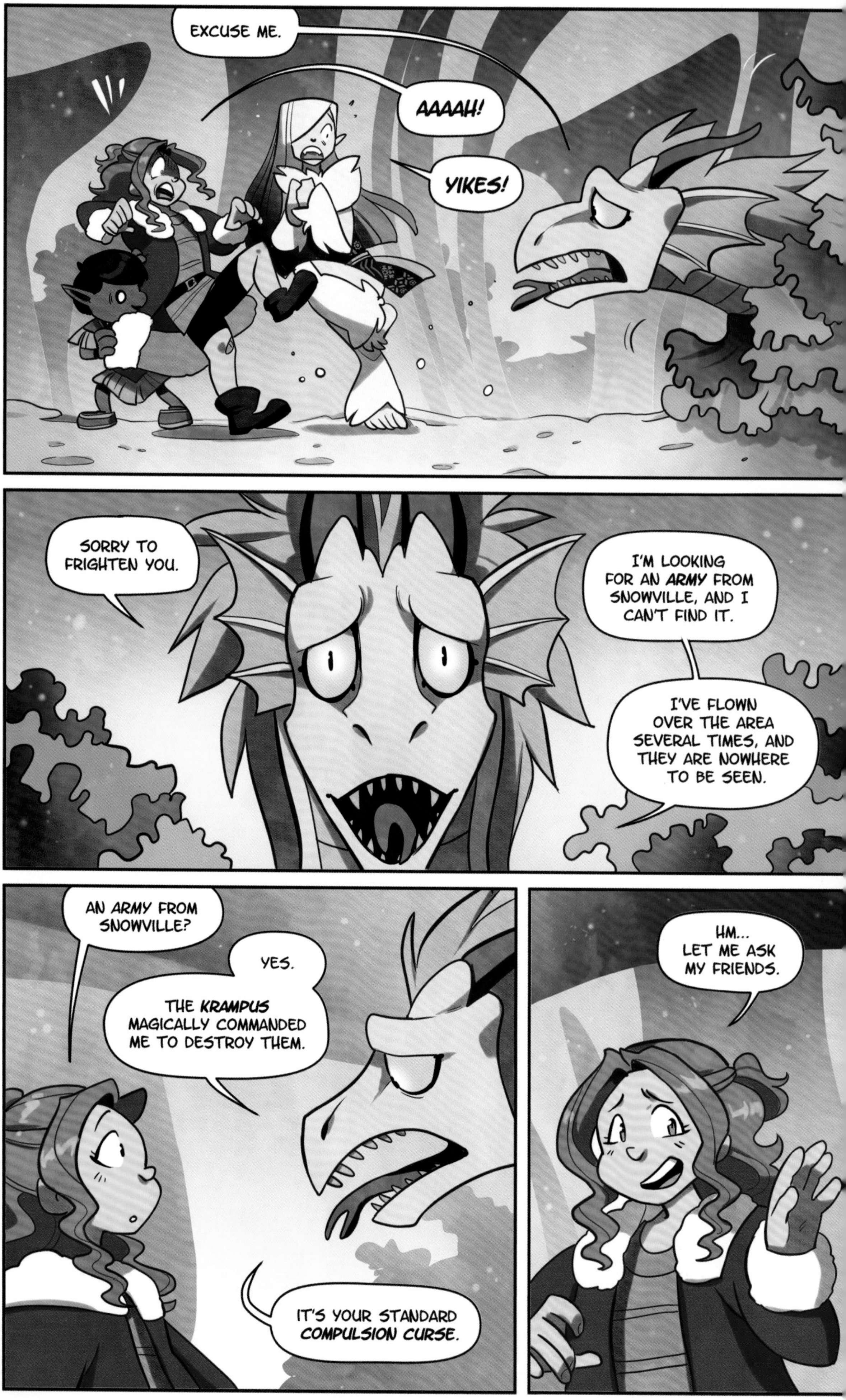
EXCUSE ME.
AAAAH!
YIKES!
SORRY TO FRIGHTEN YOU.
I'M LOOKING FOR AN ARMY FROM SNOWVILLE, AND I CAN'T FIND IT.
I'VE FLOWN OVER THE AREA SEVERAL TIMES, AND THEY ARE NOWHERE TO BE SEEN.
AN ARMY FROM SNOWVILLE?
YES.
THE KRAMPUS MAGICALLY COMMANDED ME TO DESTROY THEM.
IT'S YOUR STANDARD COMPULSION CURSE.
HM... LET ME ASK MY FRIENDS.

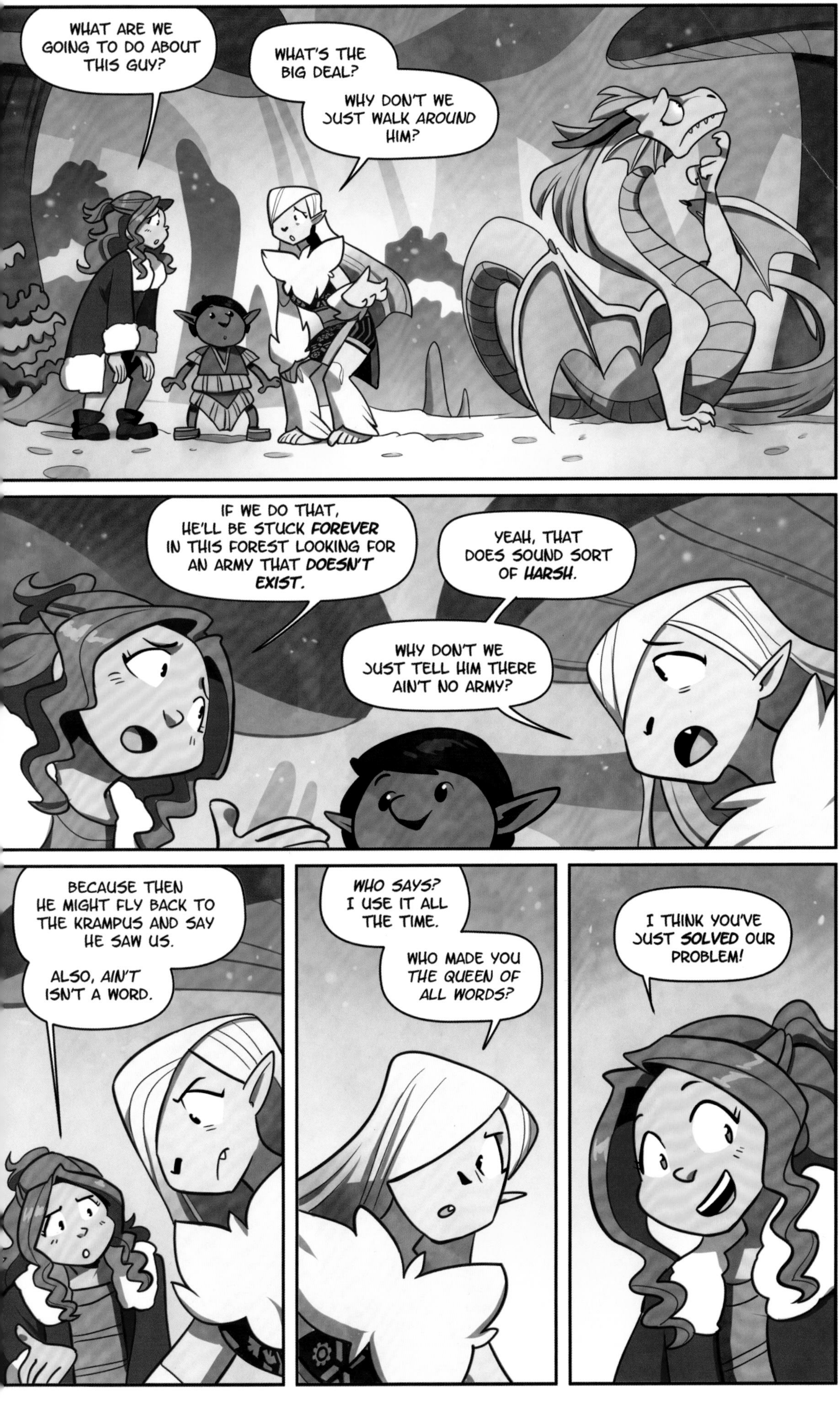

WHAT ARE WE GOING TO DO ABOUT THIS GUY?
WHAT'S THE BIG DEAL?
WHY DON'T WE JUST WALK *AROUND* HIM?
IF WE DO THAT, HE'LL BE STUCK ***FOREVER*** IN THIS FOREST LOOKING FOR AN ARMY THAT ***DOESN'T EXIST.***
YEAH, THAT DOES SOUND SORT OF ***HARSH.***
WHY DON'T WE JUST TELL HIM THERE AIN'T NO ARMY?
BECAUSE THEN HE MIGHT FLY BACK TO THE KRAMPUS AND SAY HE SAW US.
ALSO, *AIN'T* ISN'T A WORD.
WHO SAYS? I USE IT ALL THE TIME.
WHO MADE YOU THE QUEEN OF ALL WORDS?
I THINK YOU'VE JUST ***SOLVED*** OUR PROBLEM!

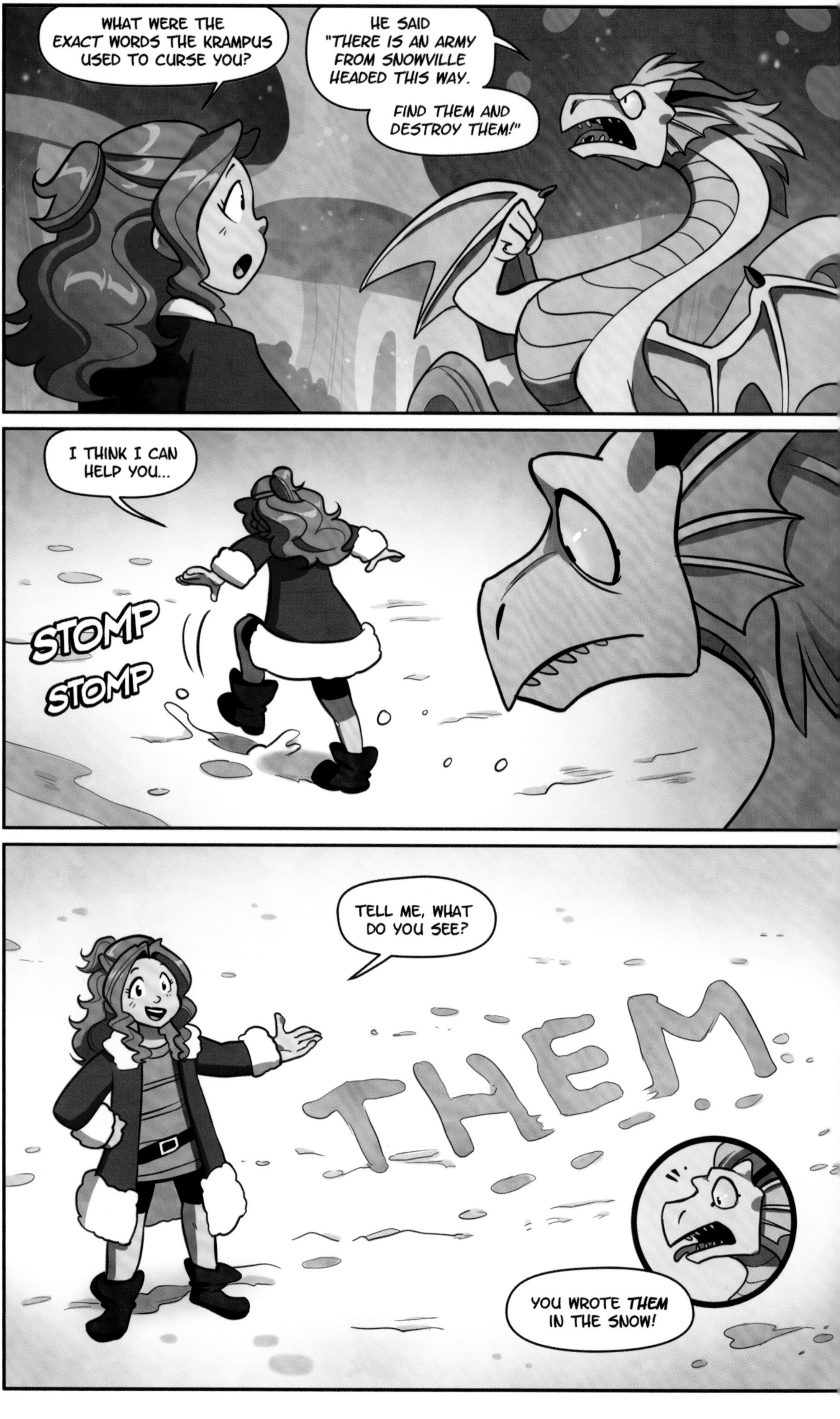
WHAT WERE THE EXACT WORDS THE KRAMPUS USED TO CURSE YOU?
HE SAID "THERE IS AN ARMY FROM SNOWVILLE HEADED THIS WAY.
FIND THEM AND DESTROY THEM!"
I THINK I CAN HELP YOU...
STOMP
STOMP
TELL ME, WHAT DO YOU SEE?
THEM
YOU WROTE THEM IN THE SNOW!

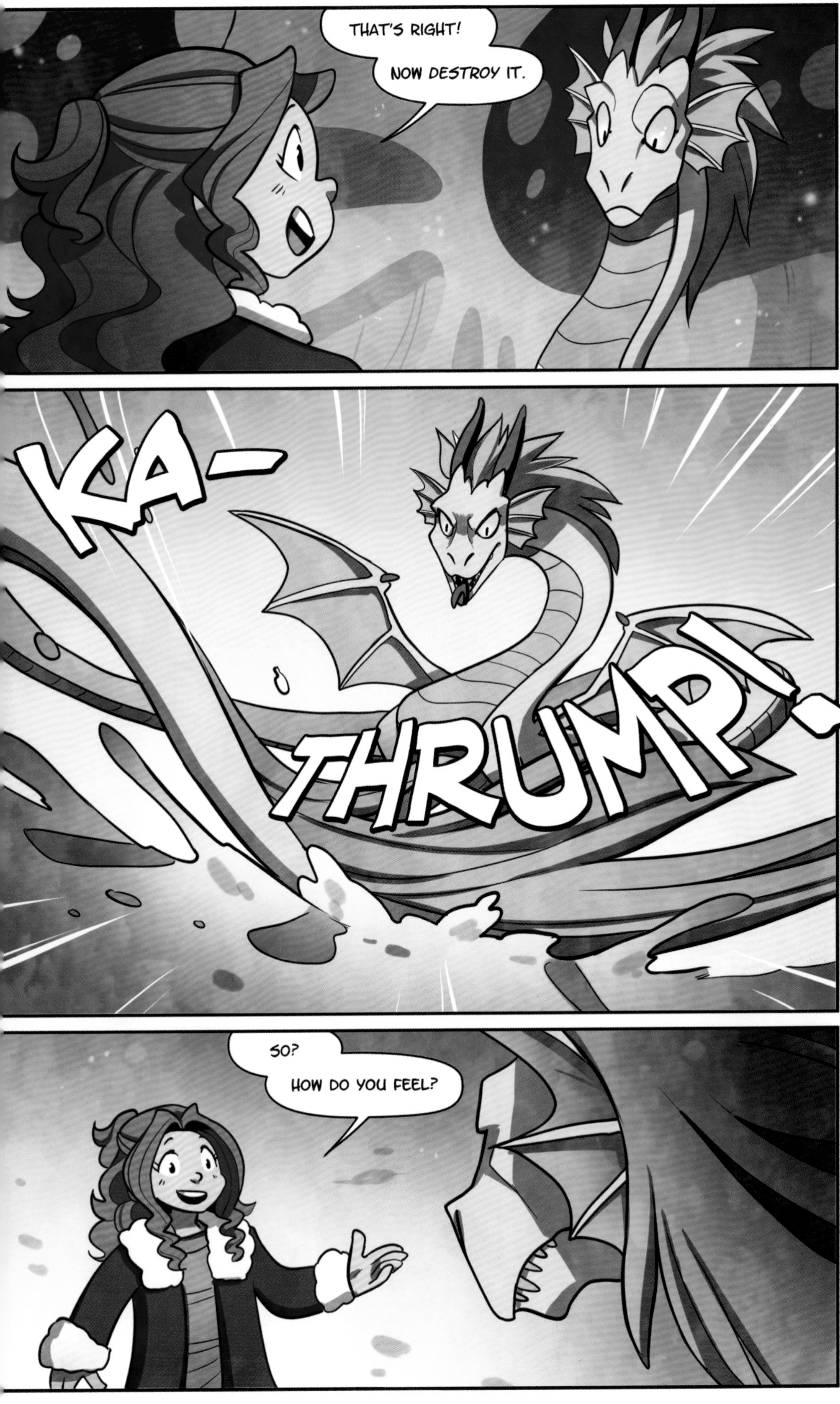
THAT'S RIGHT!
NOW DESTROY IT.
KA-
THRUMP!
SO?
HOW DO YOU FEEL?

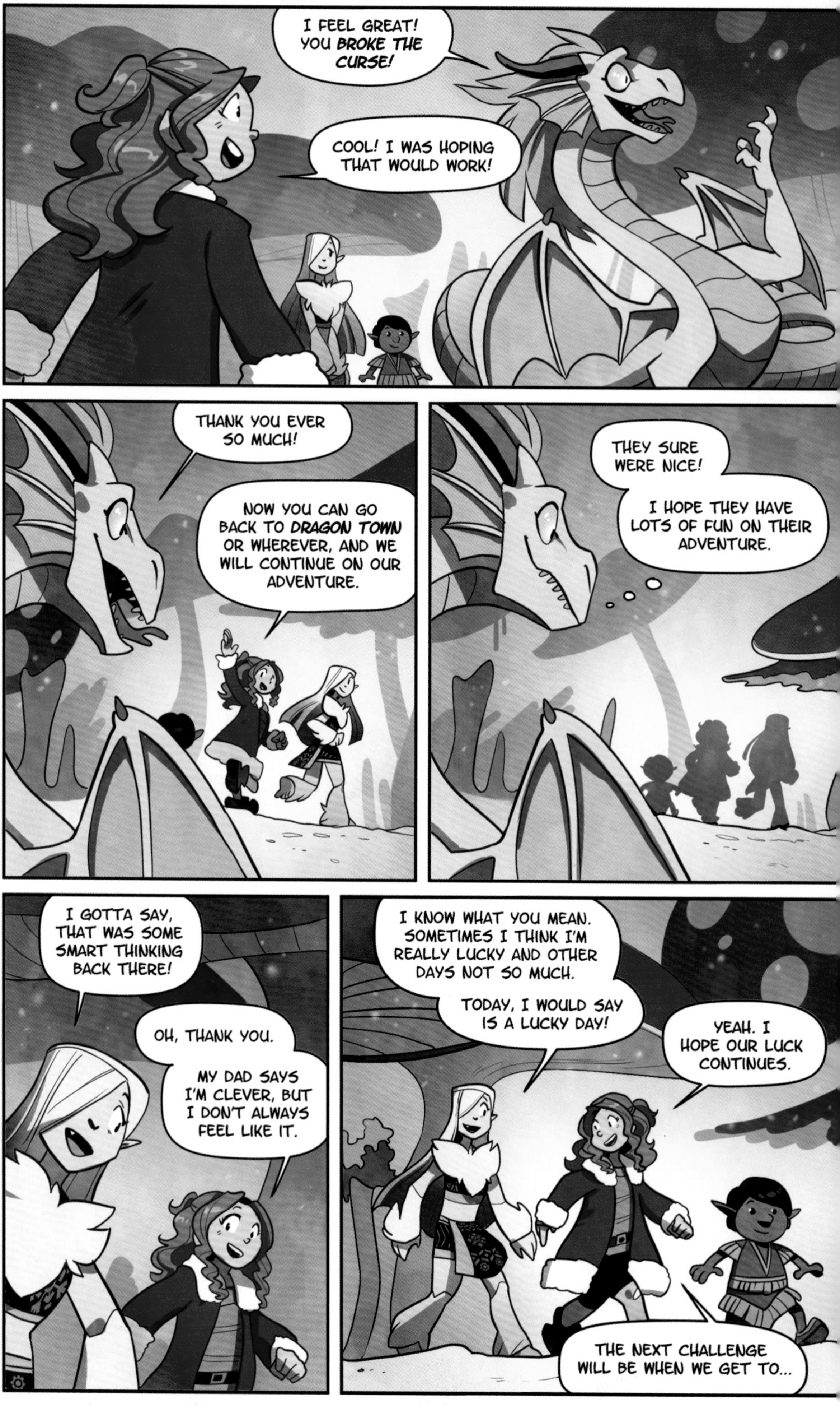

I FEEL GREAT! YOU BROKE THE CURSE!
COOL! I WAS HOPING THAT WOULD WORK!
THANK YOU EVER SO MUCH!
NOW YOU CAN GO BACK TO DRAGON TOWN OR WHEREVER, AND WE WILL CONTINUE ON OUR ADVENTURE.
THEY SURE WERE NICE!
I HOPE THEY HAVE LOTS OF FUN ON THEIR ADVENTURE.
I GOTTA SAY, THAT WAS SOME SMART THINKING BACK THERE!
OH, THANK YOU.
MY DAD SAYS I'M CLEVER, BUT I DON'T ALWAYS FEEL LIKE IT.
I KNOW WHAT YOU MEAN. SOMETIMES I THINK I'M REALLY LUCKY AND OTHER DAYS NOT SO MUCH.
TODAY, I WOULD SAY IS A LUCKY DAY!
YEAH. I HOPE OUR LUCK CONTINUES.
THE NEXT CHALLENGE WILL BE WHEN WE GET TO...

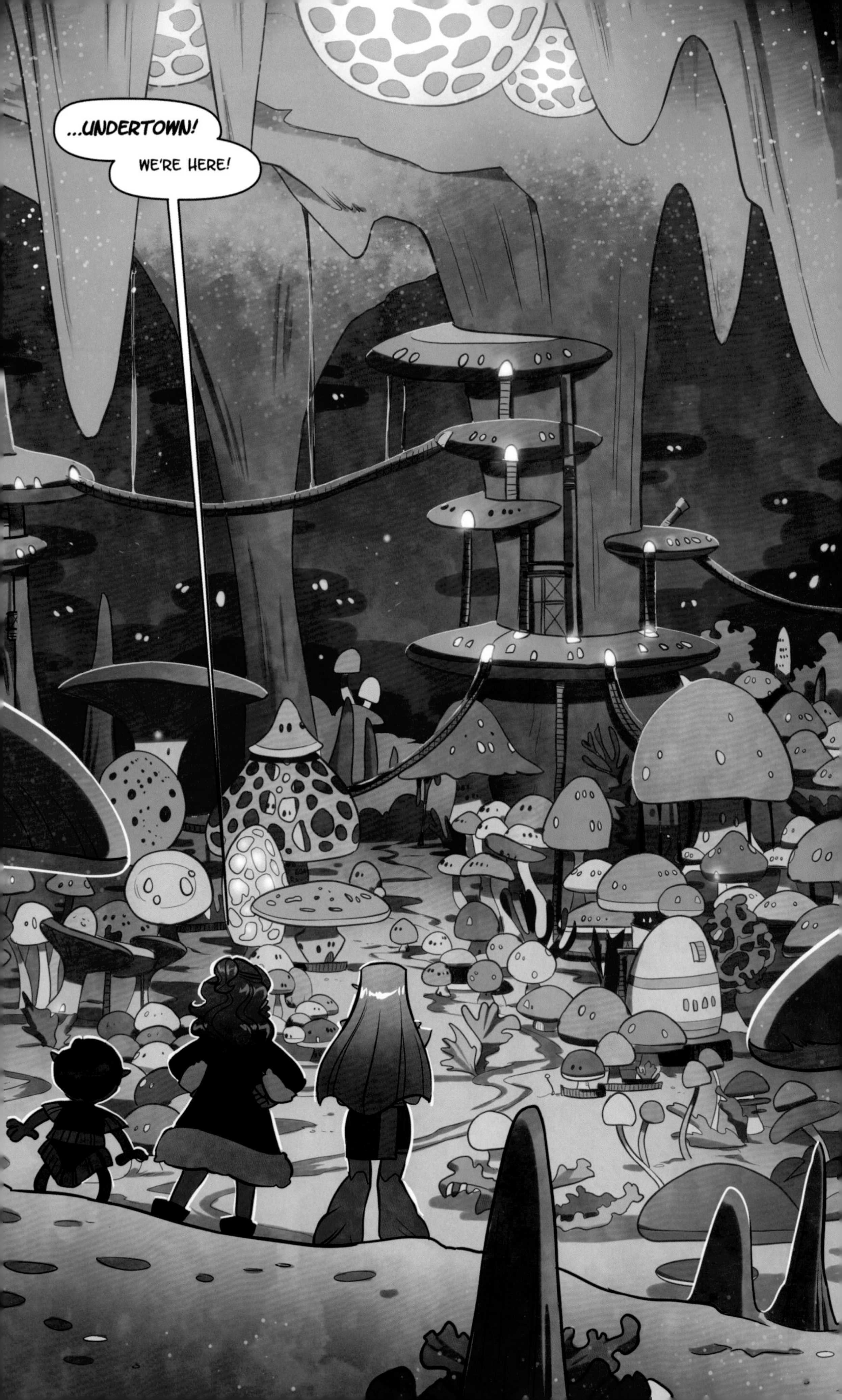
...UNDERTOWN!
WE'RE HERE!

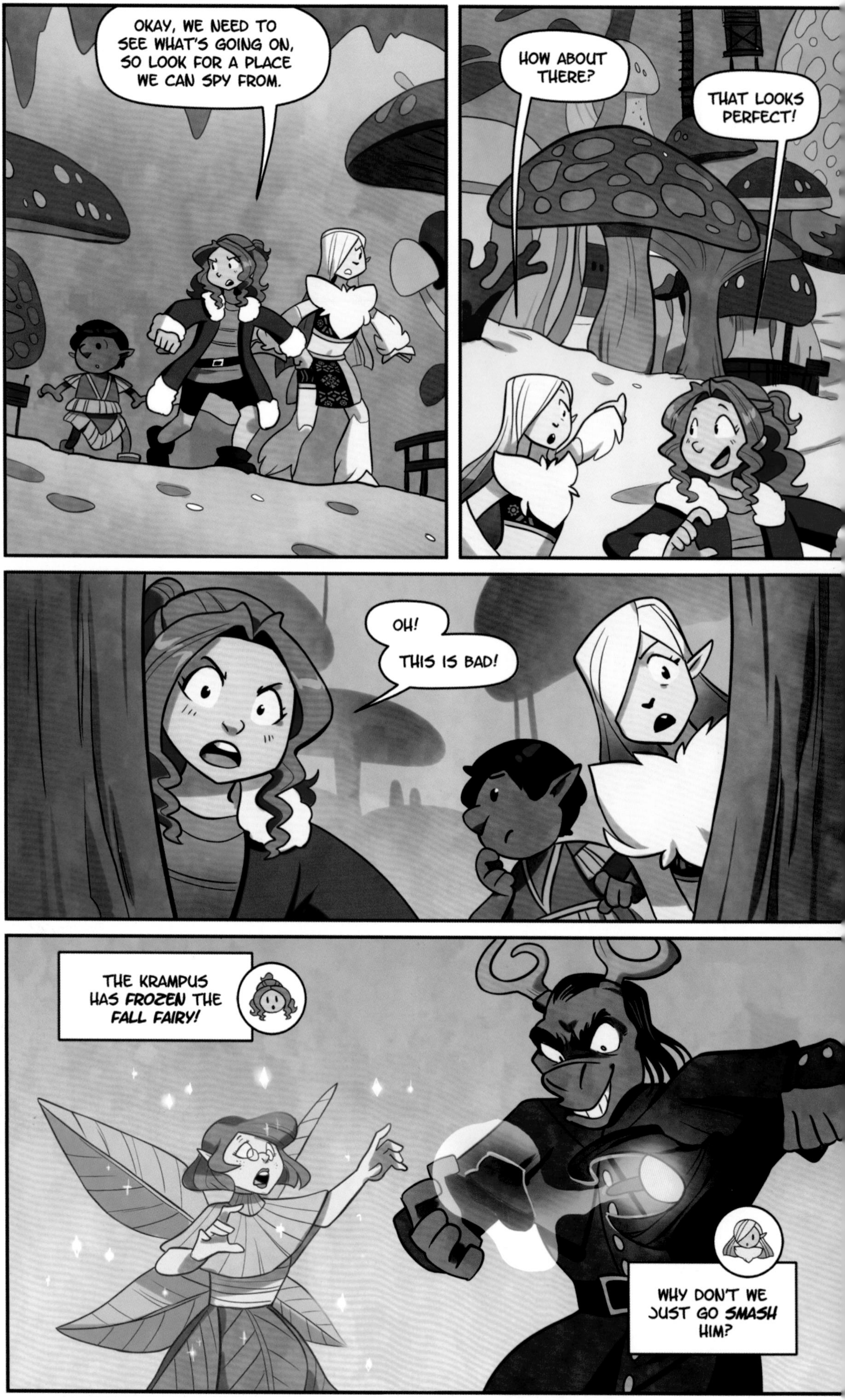
OKAY, WE NEED TO SEE WHAT'S GOING ON, SO LOOK FOR A PLACE WE CAN SPY FROM.
HOW ABOUT THERE?
THAT LOOKS PERFECT!
OH!
THIS IS BAD!
THE KRAMPUS HAS FROZEN THE FALL FAIRY!
WHY DON'T WE JUST GO SMASH HIM?

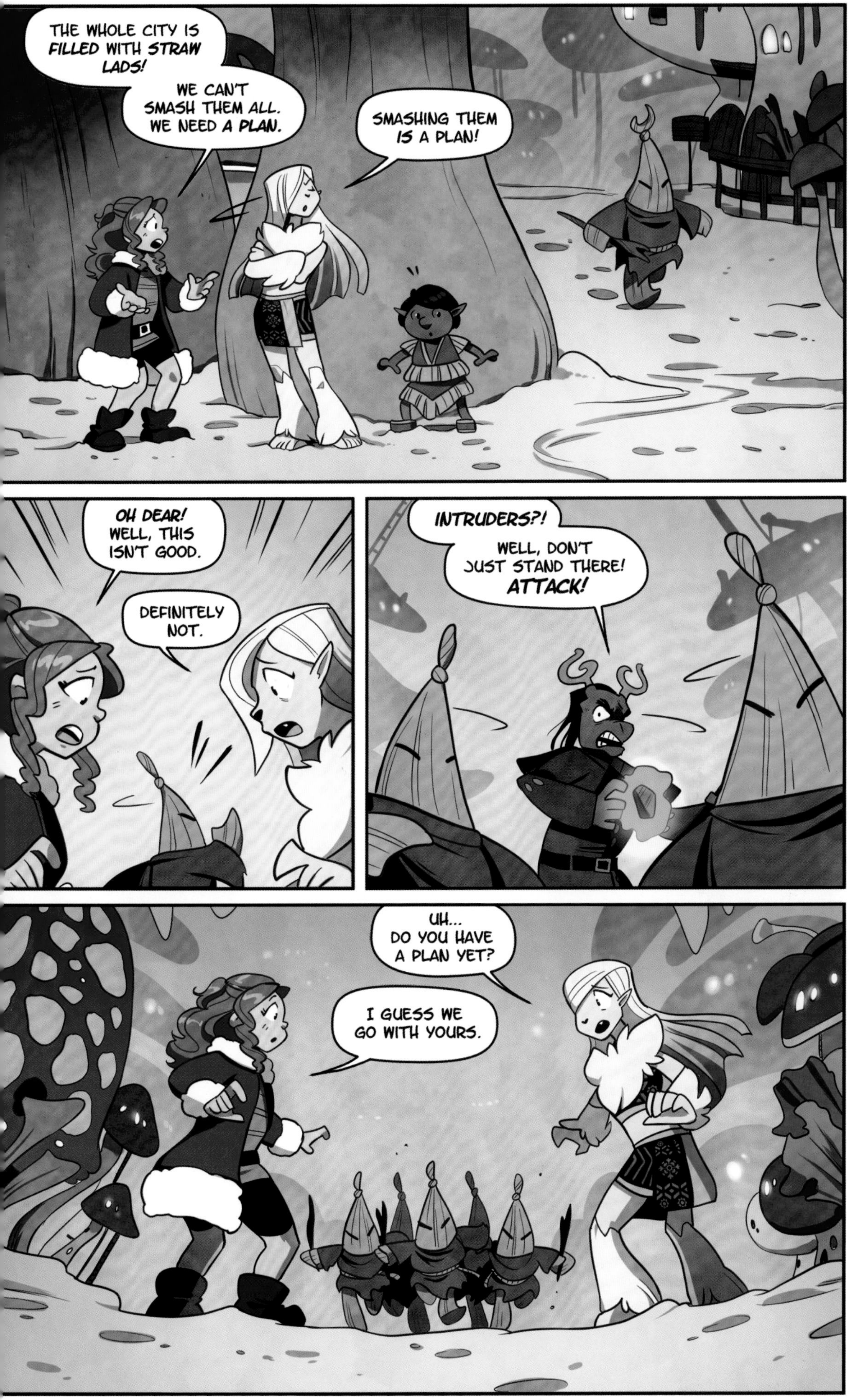
THE WHOLE CITY IS FILLED WITH STRAW LADS!
WE CAN'T SMASH THEM ALL. WE NEED A PLAN.
SMASHING THEM IS A PLAN!
OH DEAR! WELL, THIS ISN'T GOOD.
DEFINITELY NOT.
INTRUDERS?!
WELL, DON'T JUST STAND THERE! ATTACK!
UH... DO YOU HAVE A PLAN YET?
I GUESS WE GO WITH YOURS.

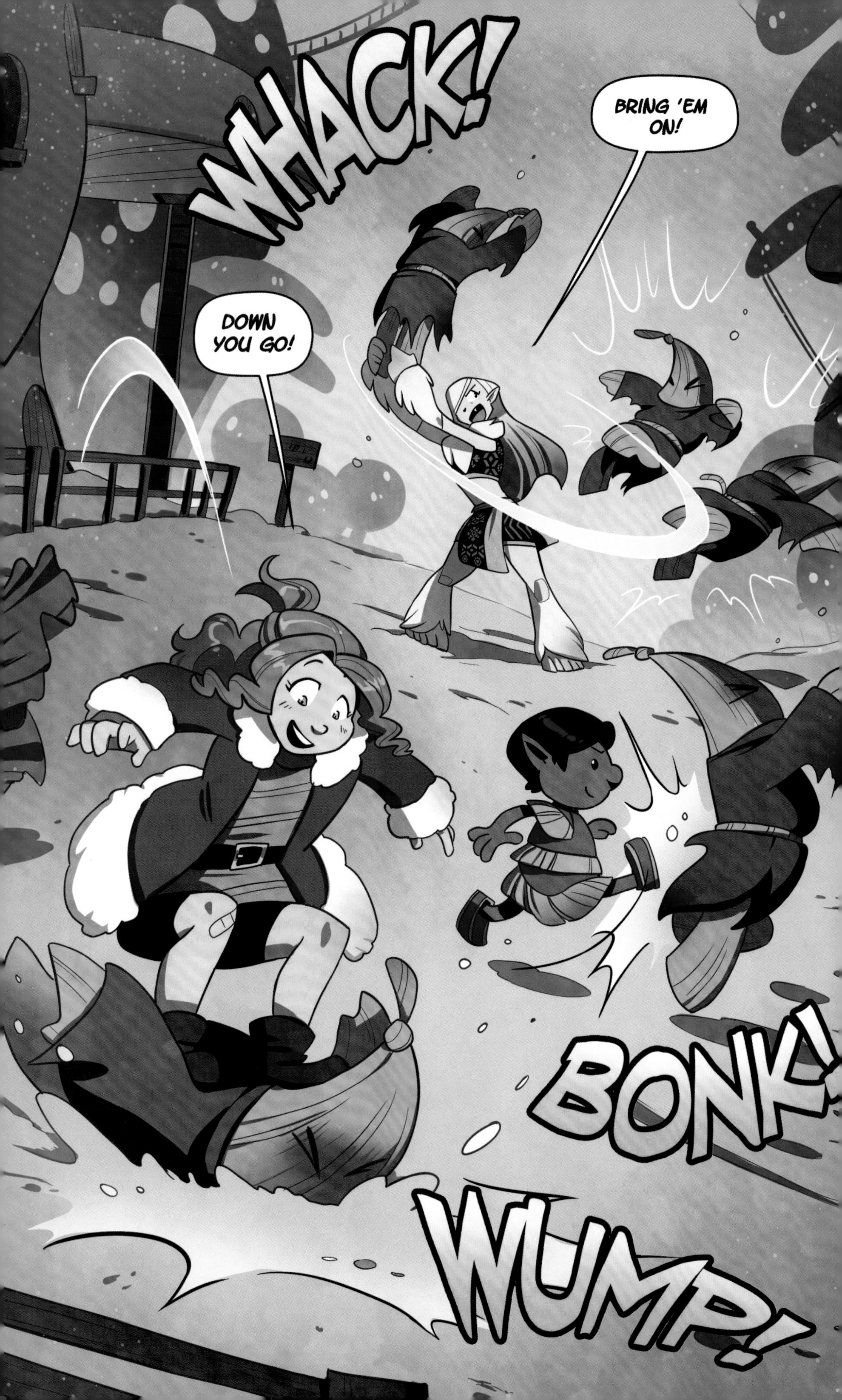
WHACK!
BRING 'EM ON!
DOWN YOU GO!
BONK!
WUMP!

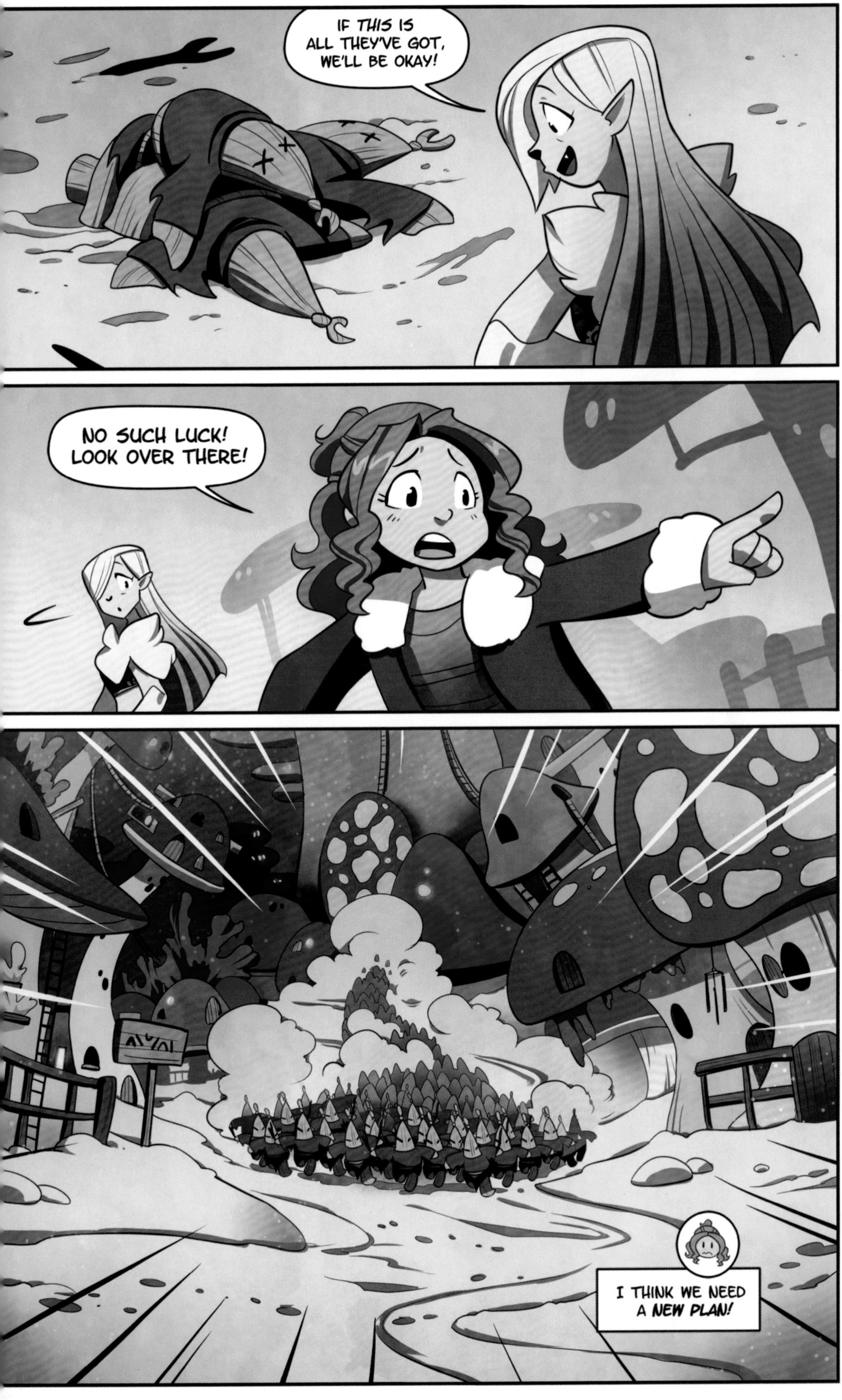
IF THIS IS ALL THEY'VE GOT, WE'LL BE OKAY!
NO SUCH LUCK! LOOK OVER THERE!
I THINK WE NEED A NEW PLAN!

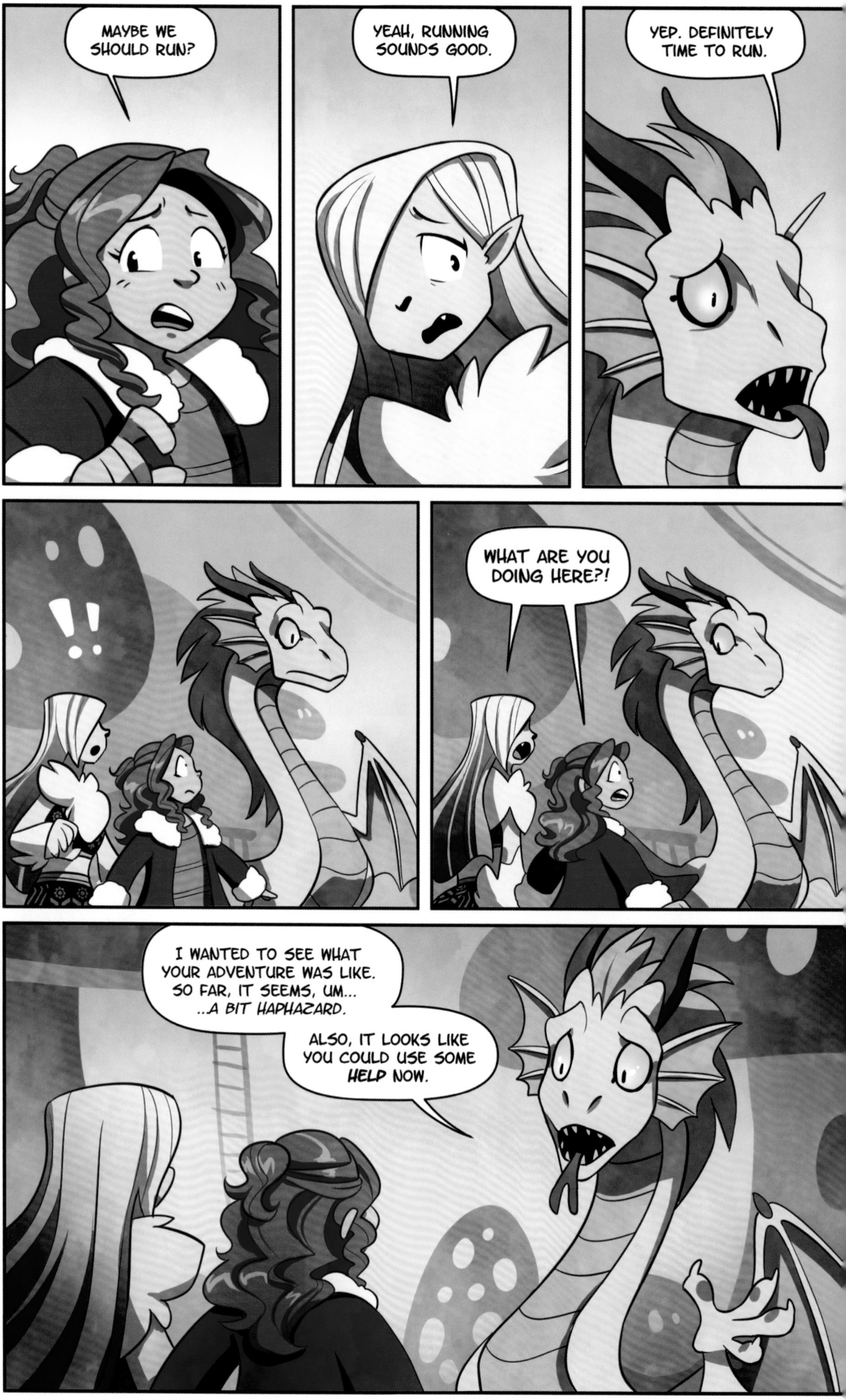

MAYBE WE SHOULD RUN?
YEAH, RUNNING SOUNDS GOOD.
YEP. DEFINITELY TIME TO RUN.
!!
WHAT ARE YOU DOING HERE?!
I WANTED TO SEE WHAT YOUR ADVENTURE WAS LIKE. SO FAR, IT SEEMS, UM... ...A BIT HAPHAZARD.
ALSO, IT LOOKS LIKE YOU COULD USE SOME HELP NOW.

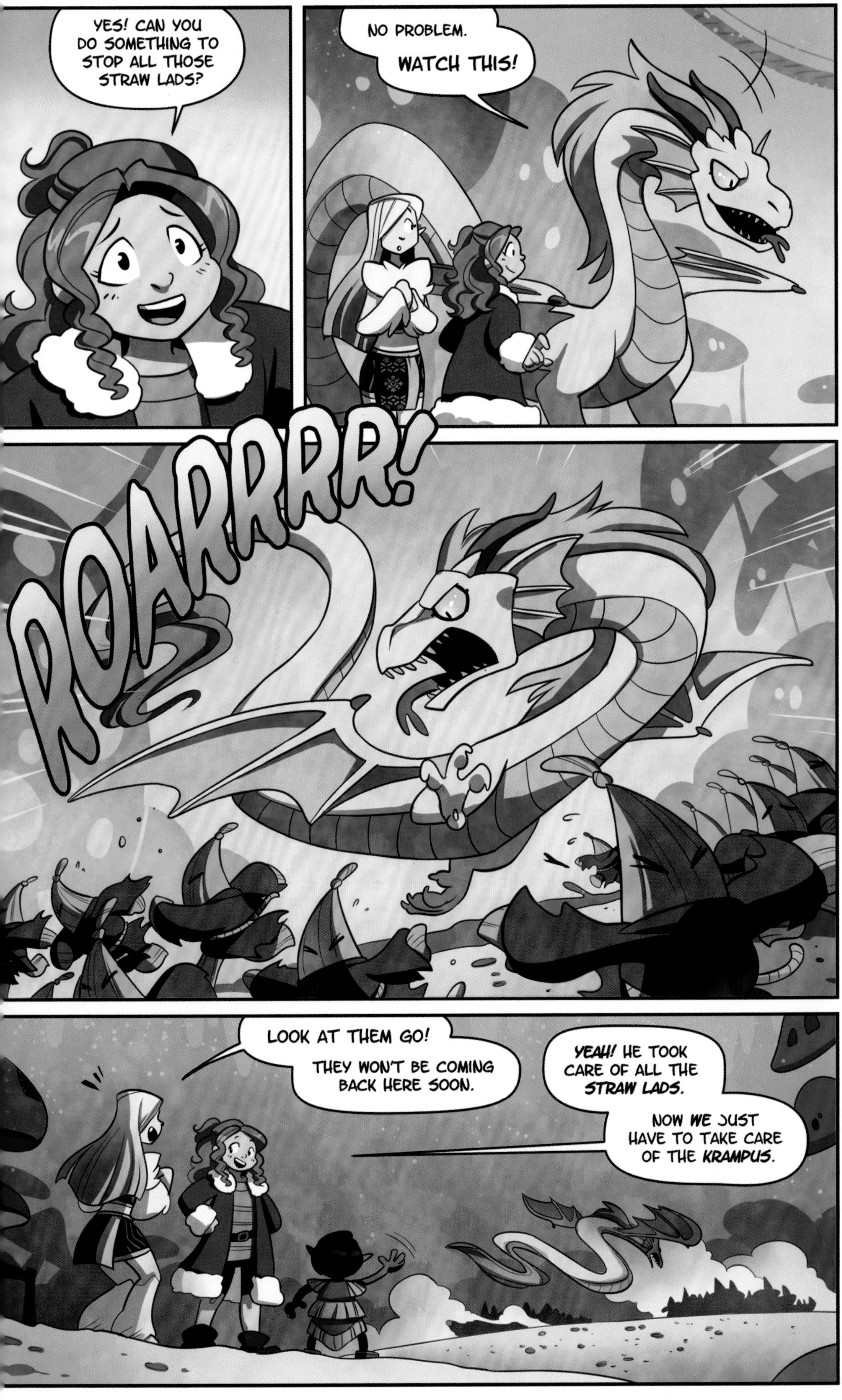
YES! CAN YOU DO SOMETHING TO STOP ALL THOSE STRAW LADS?
NO PROBLEM.
WATCH THIS!
ROARRRR!
LOOK AT THEM GO!
THEY WON'T BE COMING BACK HERE SOON.
YEAH! HE TOOK CARE OF ALL THE STRAW LADS.
NOW WE JUST HAVE TO TAKE CARE OF THE KRAMPUS.

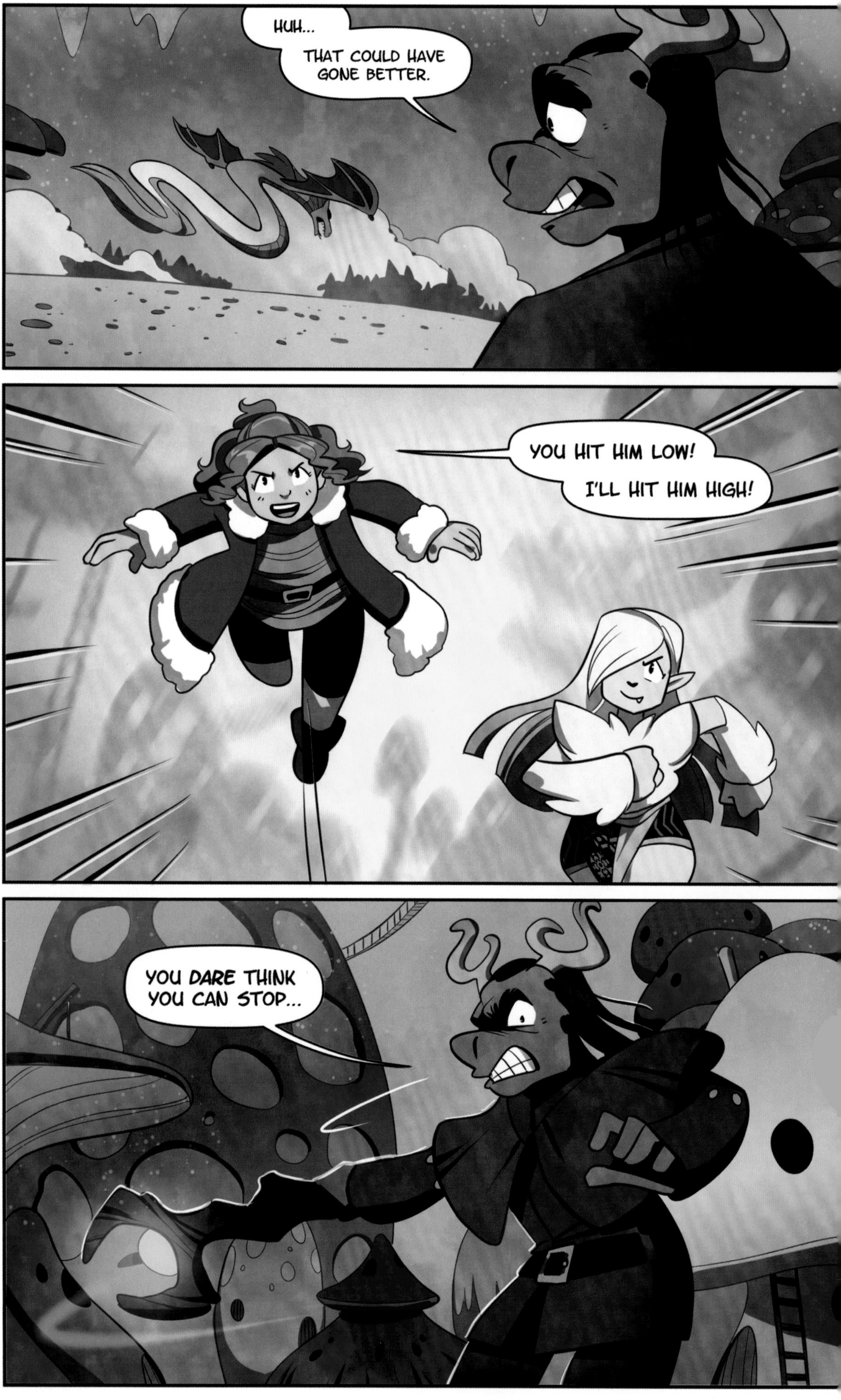
HUH...
THAT COULD HAVE GONE BETTER.
YOU HIT HIM LOW!
I'LL HIT HIM HIGH!
YOU DARE THINK YOU CAN STOP...

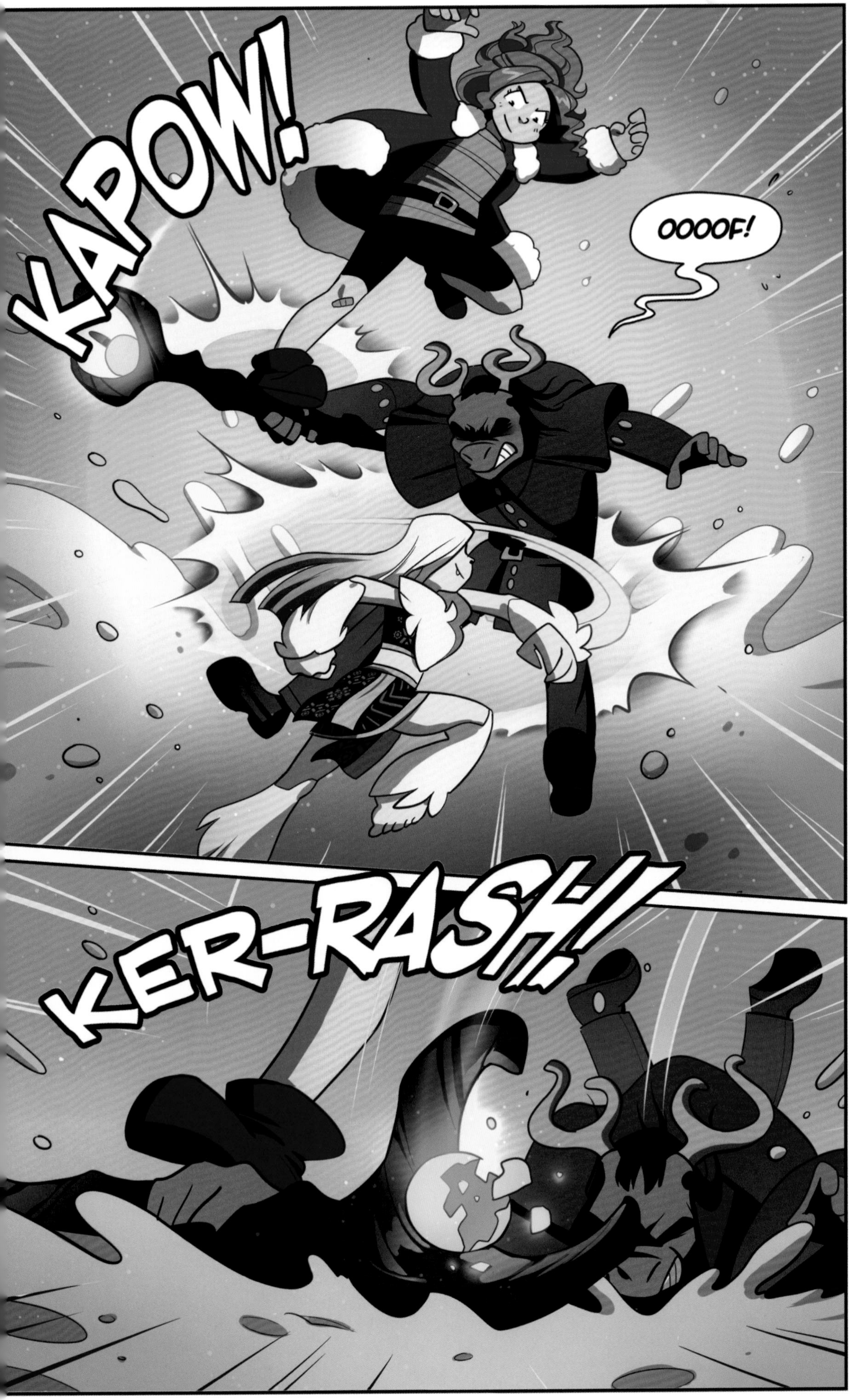
KAPOW!
OOOOF!
KER-RASH!!

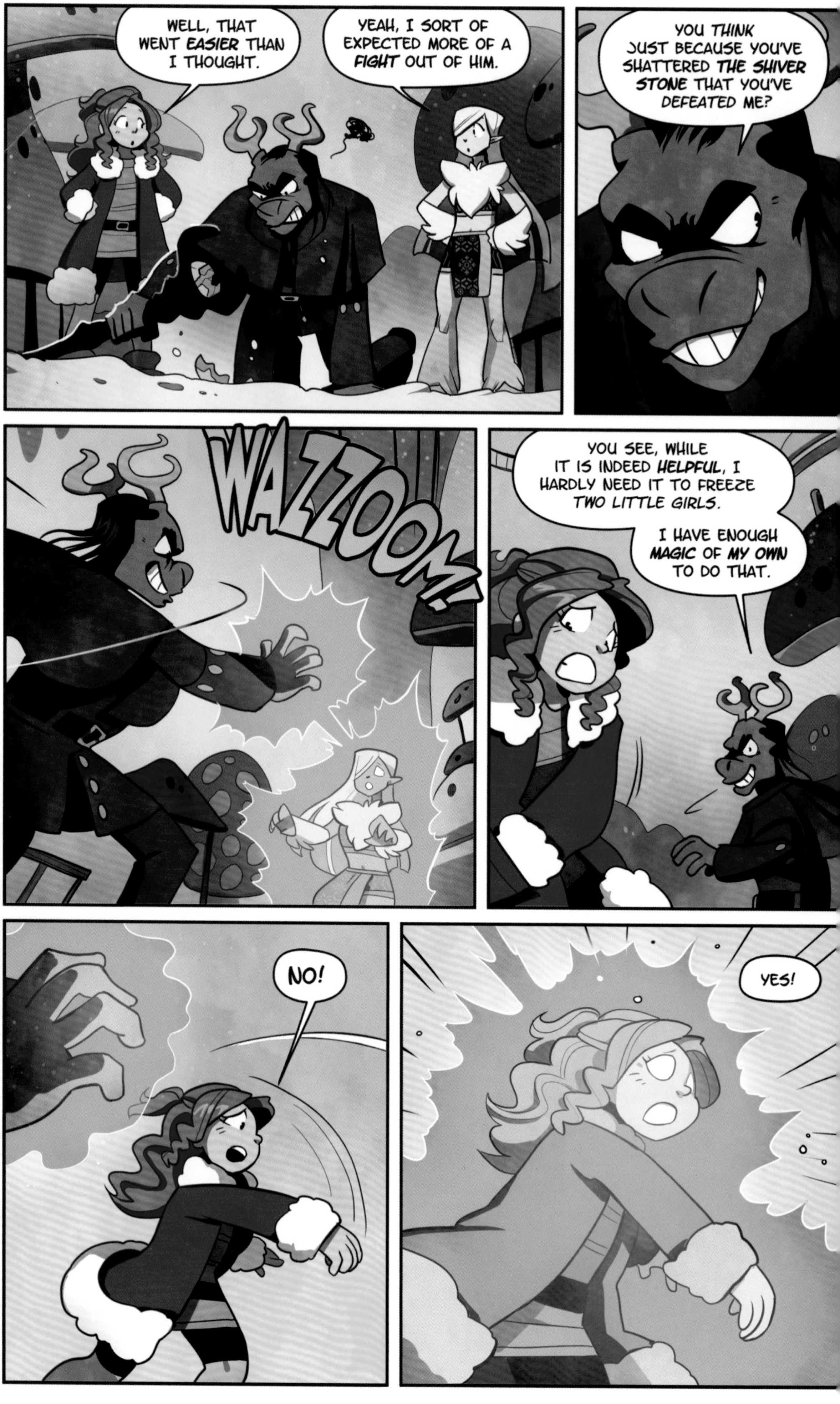
WELL, THAT WENT EASIER THAN I THOUGHT.
YEAH, I SORT OF EXPECTED MORE OF A FIGHT OUT OF HIM.
YOU THINK JUST BECAUSE YOU'VE SHATTERED THE SHIVER STONE THAT YOU'VE DEFEATED ME?
WAZZOOM!
YOU SEE, WHILE IT IS INDEED HELPFUL, I HARDLY NEED IT TO FREEZE TWO LITTLE GIRLS.
I HAVE ENOUGH MAGIC OF MY OWN TO DO THAT.
NO!
YES!

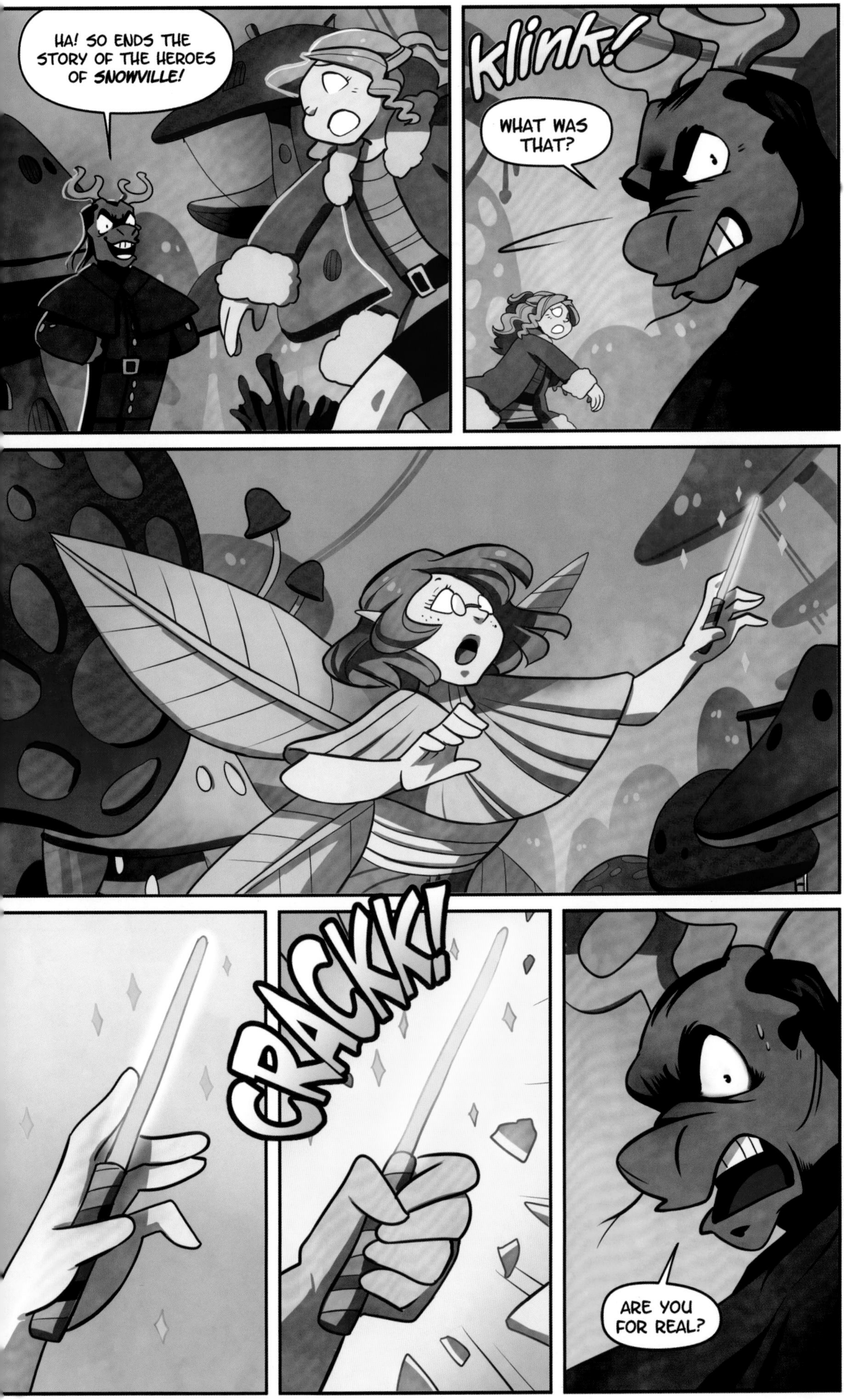
HA! SO ENDS THE STORY OF THE HEROES OF SNOWVILLE!
klink!
WHAT WAS THAT?
CRACKK!
ARE YOU FOR REAL?

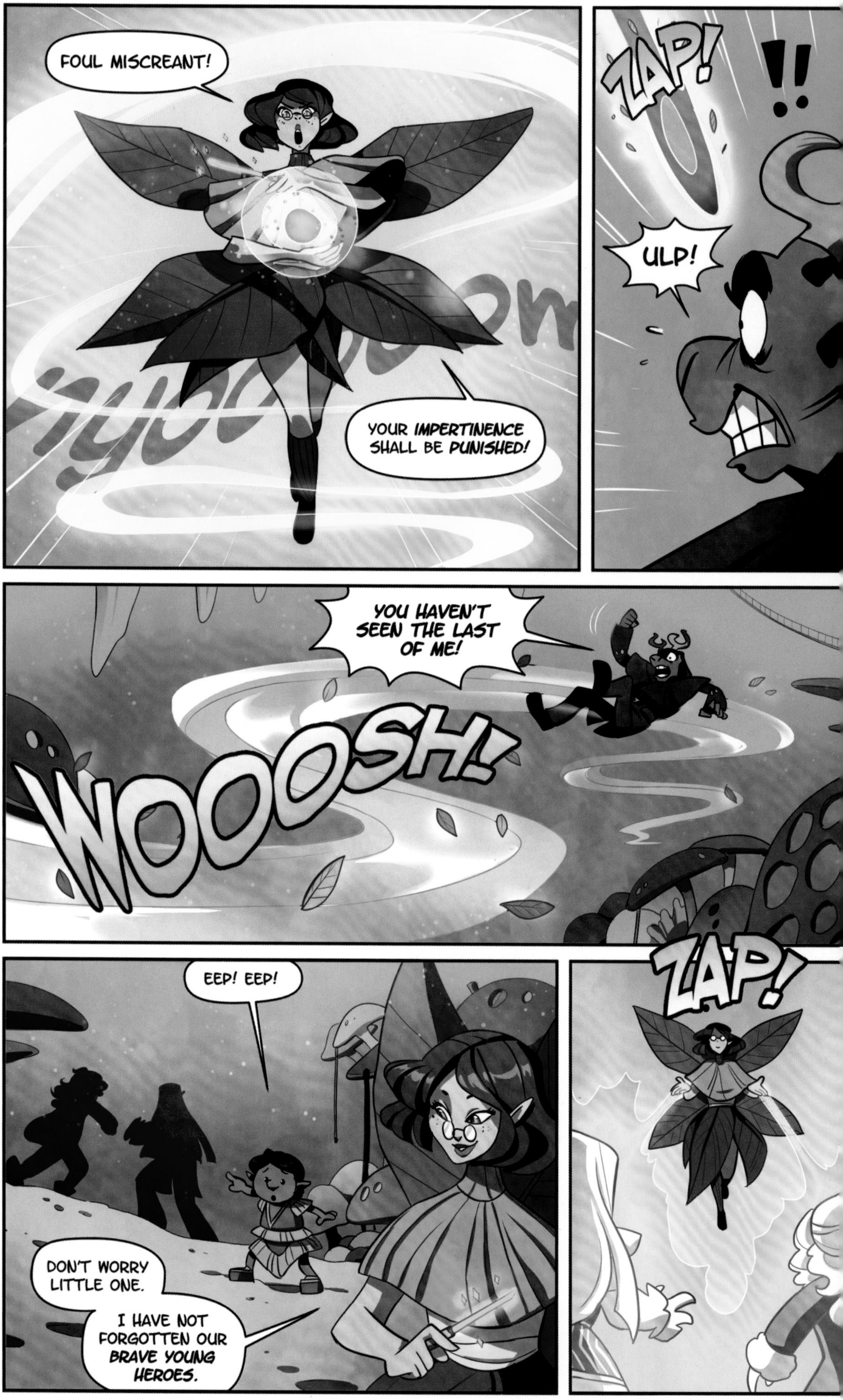
FOUL MISCREANT!
YOUR IMPERTINENCE SHALL BE PUNISHED!
ZAP!
!!
ULP!
YOU HAVEN'T SEEN THE LAST OF ME!
WOOOSH!
EEP! EEP!
DON'T WORRY LITTLE ONE.
I HAVE NOT FORGOTTEN OUR BRAVE YOUNG HEROES.
ZAP!

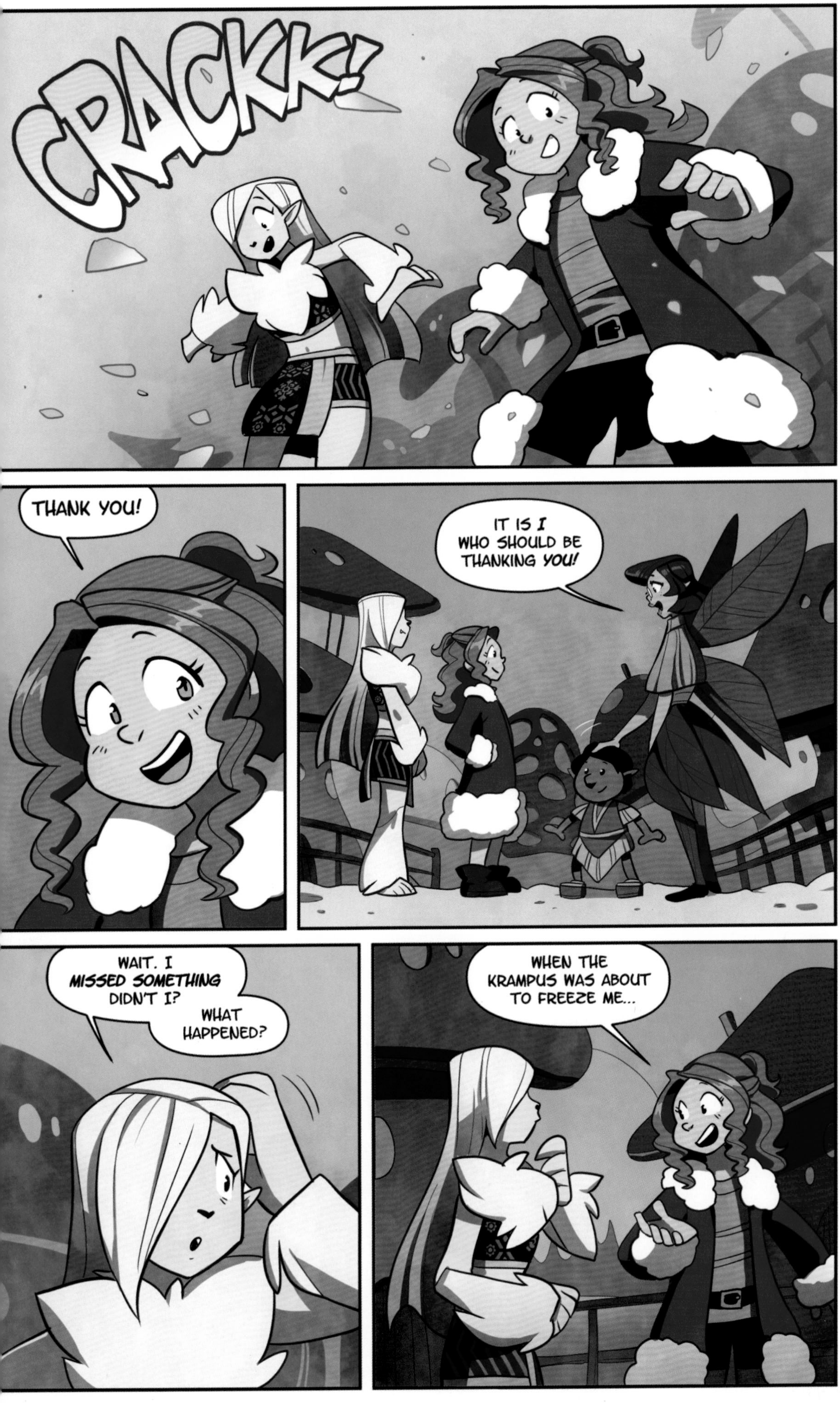
CRACKK!
THANK YOU!
IT IS I WHO SHOULD BE THANKING YOU!
WAIT. I MISSED SOMETHING DIDN'T I?
WHAT HAPPENED?
WHEN THE KRAMPUS WAS ABOUT TO FREEZE ME...

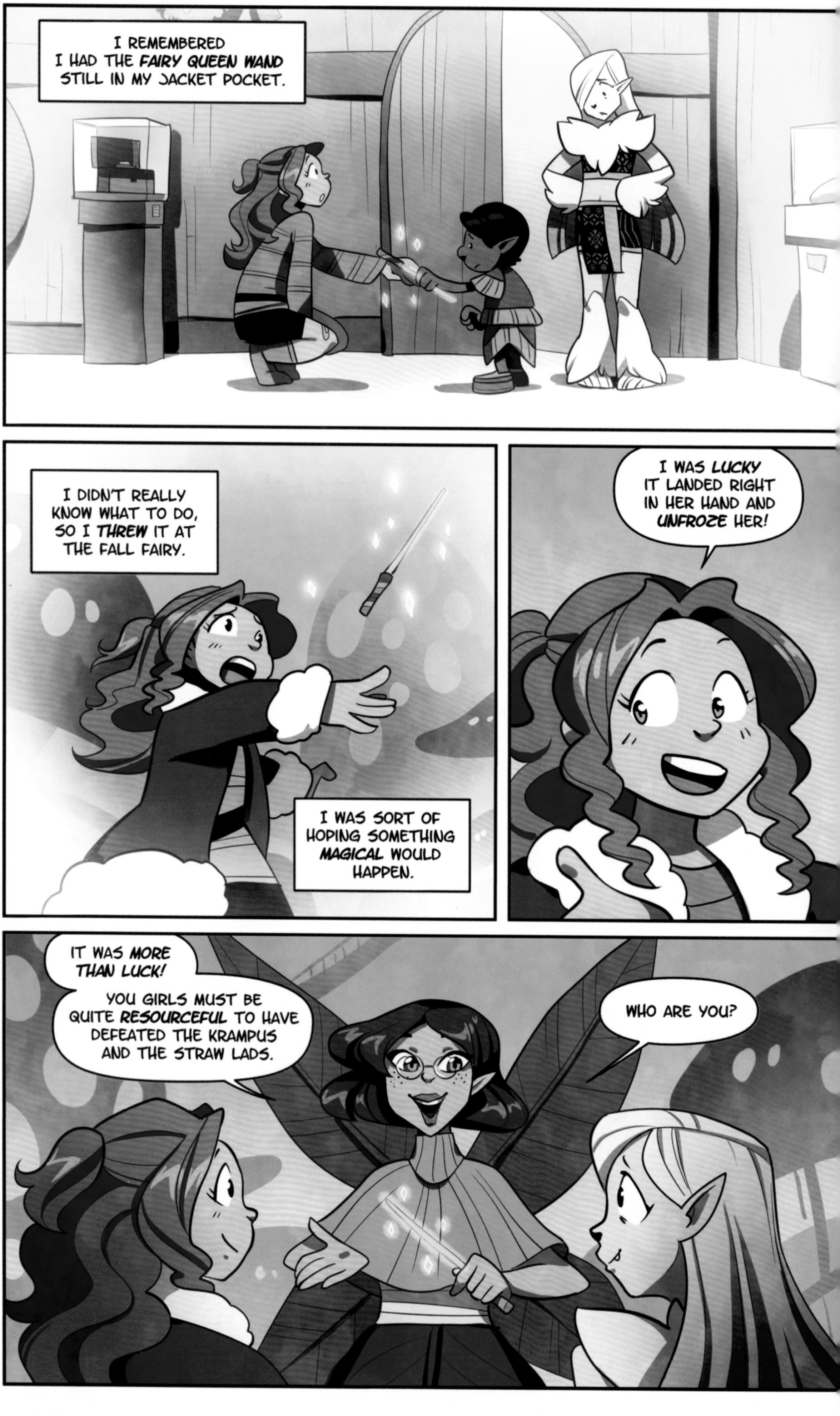
I REMEMBERED I HAD THE FAIRY QUEEN WAND STILL IN MY JACKET POCKET.
I DIDN'T REALLY KNOW WHAT TO DO, SO I THREW IT AT THE FALL FAIRY.
I WAS SORT OF HOPING SOMETHING MAGICAL WOULD HAPPEN.
I WAS LUCKY IT LANDED RIGHT IN HER HAND AND UNFROZE HER!
IT WAS MORE THAN LUCK!
YOU GIRLS MUST BE QUITE RESOURCEFUL TO HAVE DEFEATED THE KRAMPUS AND THE STRAW LADS.
WHO ARE YOU?

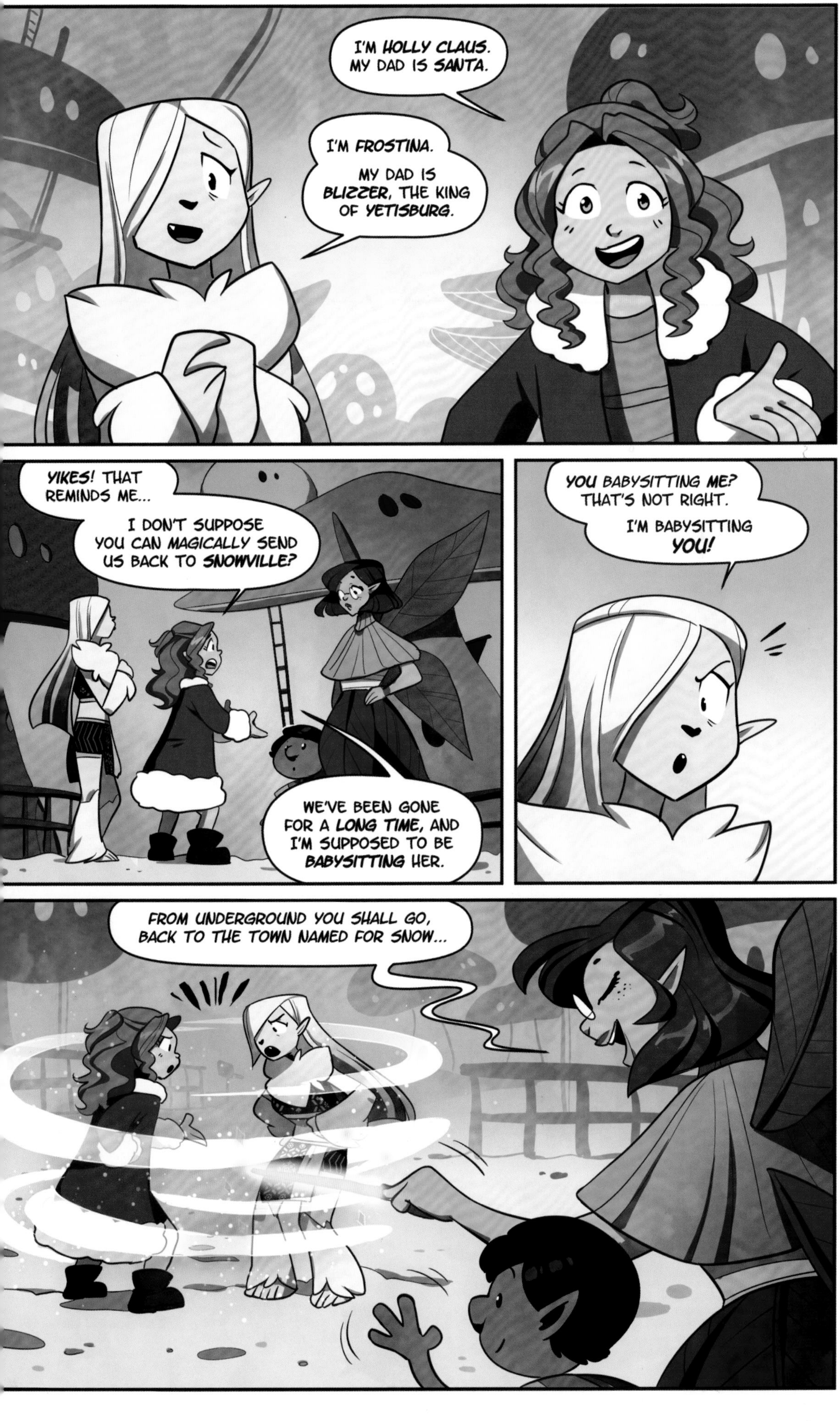
I'M HOLLY CLAUS. MY DAD IS SANTA.
I'M FROSTINA.
MY DAD IS BLIZZER, THE KING OF YETISBURG.
YIKES! THAT REMINDS ME...
I DON'T SUPPOSE YOU CAN MAGICALLY SEND US BACK TO SNOWVILLE?
WE'VE BEEN GONE FOR A LONG TIME, AND I'M SUPPOSED TO BE BABYSITTING HER.
YOU BABYSITTING ME? THAT'S NOT RIGHT.
I'M BABYSITTING YOU!
FROM UNDERGROUND YOU SHALL GO, BACK TO THE TOWN NAMED FOR SNOW...

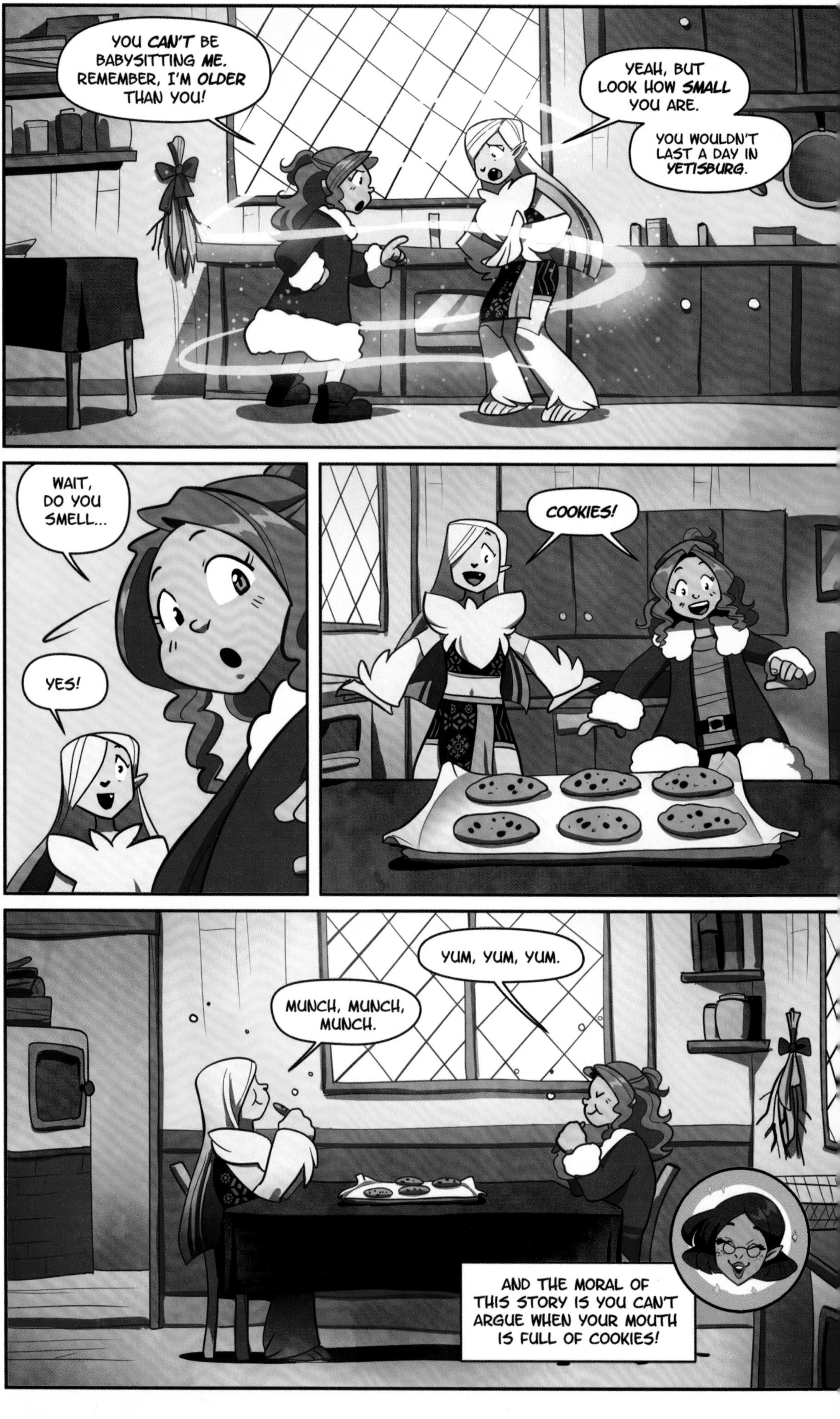
YOU CAN'T BE BABYSITTING ME. REMEMBER, I'M OLDER THAN YOU!
YEAH, BUT LOOK HOW SMALL YOU ARE.
YOU WOULDN'T LAST A DAY IN YETISBURG.
WAIT, DO YOU SMELL...
YES!
COOKIES!
MUNCH, MUNCH, MUNCH.
YUM, YUM, YUM.
AND THE MORAL OF THIS STORY IS YOU CAN'T ARGUE WHEN YOUR MOUTH IS FULL OF COOKIES!